THE IRIS PROJECT

AN ESMERALDA O`ROURKE ADVENTURE

BY K.L.A. HYATT

Chapter 1

Beijing

June 12, 1959

I longed to lean back in my chair and rub the back of my neck, shake my hair loose. My suit had moved into a very irritating position and I really wanted to fix it. That was the problem with the full-spell glamour suits, they always crept up somewhere uncomfortable.

My fingers hesitated over the abacus as I glanced around the bare, badly-lit room in search of the supervisor, wondering if I could risk a 15 second break for some quick adjustments. Just then the hateful man slammed a small paddle down on the side of my desk.

"Chin lo, if there is no life threatening reason for your hands to be still, I suggest you get back to work." The supervisor, a short man in his 40s, continued his walk up to the front of the room. I didn't dare watch him, I leaned over my paperwork feeling the silent snickers and half smiles that my coworkers were directing at me.

Pursing my lips, I got back into the job at hand. While quickly calculating, by aid of the abacus, the long rows of numbers on the pages before me, I couldn't help but think that this was the most tedious and worst assignment I had ever had. Two solid weeks of days filled with accounting and the accompanying clack of a roomful of abacuses was really taking a toll on my nerves.

And what was I looking for? A needle in a haystack. Mistress's ridiculously vague instructions: "We are trying to find evidence that the Arcanimus are providing weapons for the Republic of China. If they are, there will be evidence of payment going through the government's central accounting office. Find it."

Find it, ha! I thought. After two weeks, I had only come across two items of any interest. A large payment to a small bank in Syria and a similar sum to a Gobi Animus Co. with an address in Patagonia. Two hot spots of Arcanimus activity. I had dutifully recorded both entries with my Witness glass, but neither bit of information was conclusive.

I also was beginning to feel the language charm wear off and I didn't have the ready means to renew it. The Chinese characters were slowly losing their comprehensibility. Every time I opened my mouth I was sure a Chinese-English hybrid of gibberish was going to come out.

I stifled a sigh. Better apply myself—the sooner I found concrete evidence, the sooner I would be able to go home.

After my day of work was through, I was once again on the noisy, smelly streets of Beijing and feeling much better. Sitting at that cramped desk for 10 hours a day was unbearable. I couldn't imagine how those poor fellows who worked along side me could do it day after day for most of their lives.

But they were none of my concern. I was glad it was only temporary for me. Walking back to the boarding house where I was staying while undercover, I decided that I was hungry enough to enjoy even the most revolting meal served by my landlady and that I would hog the communal bath for a long time in order to get out of my disguise and relax.

Dinner was as disgusting as I thought it would be. Sitting at a long bench and plank table with my fellow boarders, I wolfed down the rice and slimy vegetables before me. I tried not to think of the filet mignon at Flaubert's in New York, but I was feeling malnourished after eating the same slimy vegetables and rice everyday.

Following several of the other boarders, I climbed the stairs to the bare, minimalist room I shared with three men. Each roommate had one corner of the room in which to place their belongings and in which to face in order to get some semblance of privacy. I laid down on my small cot and stared at the stained ceiling already disgusted with the smelly men I was confined with. Two of my roommates started playing a game with dice. The fourth had not returned.

I knew that there would be a line for the bath this early in the evening and decided to wait a few hours so that I would, hopefully, be the last person. I lay on the bed going over the scanty bit of evidence that I had come across so far. There were the two previous payments to suspect companies or individuals, but that afternoon I had added a third item to my list.

I had come across a paid-in-cash invoice for a large number of something called Medallon X113 from a company called A.R.C. Corporation located in Basil, Switzerland. It seemed odd that I had never heard of anything by that name, but the name of the company made it very suspicious. I had dutifully recorded the invoice.

Nearly dozing off, I sat up abruptly. I checked the time on my cheap wristwatch and saw that it was nearly 10 o'clock. The perfect time to get in line for a wash. I leaned over the small bureau and pulled open the top drawer to retrieve clean under garments and my toiletries. As I made to leave the room, one of my roommates called out, "Hey Chin, did your mama raise you in a whorehouse to make you that fastidious."

I turned sharply on the man who had flung the insult. He was the oldest of my roommates. Wearing only his undershorts and scratching his big belly, he laughed heartily at his own joke. The young man seated across from him never took his eyes off the dice. I didn't say a word even as my eyes flared with anger. I left the room quickly. Insults and outrages flew threw my head, but I couldn't risk saying anything. The language charm was definitely losing its strength. It had sounded to me as if the old geezer had said "Knock your Chin low, the dog fed you to the grass which is why you dress in mauve." The words had taken a few seconds, much longer than it should, to descramble in my mind.

I sighed as I got in line for the bath. There were only two men in front of me. I wondered if I would have enough time and privacy to renew the language charm that night. After that last flub, I knew that it probably wouldn't last through the next day.

The last man in line ahead of me finally exited the bathroom, the attendant was already fast asleep. I waved a hand over the boy's head, thinking the charms for peace and rest, ensuring a long and peaceful sleep for the boy. The door did not have a lock, so I placed a chair in front of it. Looking around I saw that bathroom was a mess. For each of the men who had used it had splashed water and soap grime everywhere. By the looks of things, many of them had been very dirty to begin with. The bathroom attendant, my landlady's youngest son, was only responsible for keeping track of who visited the room and filling the tub with the maximum 4 inches of water. Good thing that I was prepared to make do without the attendant.

Looking at the filthy tub, I held my hand out, fingers spread. Concentrating I waved my hand a bit then pinched my fingers together. I tugged with my hand as if I were tugging at a cord that wouldn't come free. Then I moved my hand from one side of the tub to the other and flicked my fingers to the other side. The spell had peeled away all of layers of dirt and grime that ringed the tub. Coming free it flew through the air and landed with a splat against the far wall and from there oozed down into a filthy puddle on the floor.

I concentrated again on the tub and watched it as it began to fill with very hot, soapy water. The water was far too clean to be from the old taps fixed to the wall behind the tub. Not exactly by-the-book for an undercover agent, but I was too tired, dirty, and cross to care.

Smiling to myself, I began to undress. Starting at the crown of my head, I began to peel off my skin. As if I were peeling a banana, I took off the glamour that made the 5 foot 8 inch-tall European-featured woman into a 5 foot 2 inch-tall pudgy Asian male. Stepping out of the superfine, fake skin, I stretched my arms tall above my head and rotated my neck, loosening up my shoulder muscles. I shook my hair free and rubbed my face. I draped the suit over the back of a chair. It laid rumpled like a deflated person, the short hair standing on end nearly touched the floor.

I climbed into the bubble-filled water. I had bathed within the confines of the glamour for the previous two weeks. As the suit could be hot, cleanliness was a key factor in these long-term undercover assignments. One wouldn't want to give oneself away by an unpleasant personal odor. I knew I was taking a great risk by bathing undisguised, it didn't stop me. Instead I luxuriated in the soft warm bubbles.

Knowing I would have to renew the language spell sometime during the night I was considering the few places in the building that would offer enough privacy for me to work the spell. Language and communication spells weren't difficult, just time consuming and noisy. I was considering paying a visit to my own apartment in New York to work the spell when I heard a sliding noise. It sounded suspiciously like a chair being slid across the floor.

I turned my head in the direction of the door. The chair I had used as a failsafe was fully two feet from the door. As I looked up, I saw the door open a crack and a face concealed in shadow watching me. When my eyes met those of the spy, the door shut quickly and I heard feet padding softly away.

From the chair's position, I knew it had to have been moved, not with someone's hands or even a tool slid under the door, but by magic.

"Damn it all to Hades," I quietly cursed. I quickly climbed from the tub. Putting my open palm out in front of me I said, "Robe." An instant later a bright orange robe appeared in my hand. Appalled at the color, I quickly put it on tucking the glamour in to the belt. Within 10 seconds of the closing of the door, I was following the spy.

The bathroom was at the end of a long hallway. The stairwell was at the opposite end. I had not heard another door open or shut, so I was certain the spy had traversed the length of the hallway. As I moved stealthy towards the far end I used my free hand to begin a shield spell, calling the symbols of defense and stealth, and holding it out in front of me. Near to the end of the hallway, I slowed down. For a split second someone poked their head around the corner. The next second I heard someone taking the staircase. I gave pursuit.

I knew that I was likely being lead into a trap, but if I had any say in the matter, I wouldn't let that spy get the better of me.

When I reached the stairway landing, I saw that the spy had taken the stairs upwards. I knew where the spy was headed. The roof. It was the best vantage point from which to make a leap. I was on the second floor of a four story building. Deciding instantly what I must do, I hesitated at the landing and reached into one of the inner pockets of the glamour. I removed a small medallion and slung it around my neck using the cord that was attached.

Next I waved my hand over the rumpled glamour and sent it to my apartment in New York. Without another second to lose, I tightened the belt on the ugly robe and ran up the stairs in pursuit.

I had barely made the fourth floor landing when I heard the door to the rooftop bump close. A smug smile of satisfaction crossed my mouth as I continued to the roof. I was right. The spy had made for the rooftop and it was a trap.

Just behind the door to roof, I stopped to reach for my magic—my full connection to magic. I closed my eyes and gripped the medallion about my neck and in my mind described the protection I would need as I walked through the rough wooden door in front of me.

Feeling the pulse of the magic flow, I reached for the door handle before me and pushed. As soon as I was beyond the door frame on the flat roof, a flash of gold light tore through the night. It came straight for me and I turned to face it, whipping my shield spell in front of me. Just inches away from contact it suddenly rebounded as if it had hit an invisible trampoline. It flew back from where it came, overtaking, with surprise, the person who had flung it.

I saw a figure dressed in dark clothes lit up by the light of the magic fire ball. It struck the figure and I could just see the body rolling along the roof. In what certainly should be too little time, the person had stopped herself and flung another ball of light at me.

This time I was even more prepared. Walking towards it, I reached through my shield and caught the ball absorbing it into my hand. The dark figure threw three balls in succession as she tried to back away.

I easily caught them all. I held the third ball letting it hover above my hand to cast a bright glow across the rooftop. I was only a few feet away from the spy by that time. The only feature visible underneath the dark mask she wore were her dark, fearless eyes.

The next few seconds were of essence. I quickly calculated the situation. If the dark figure were given more than 5 seconds of inactivity, she would vanish and I would never know who she was. I threw the ball of magic at the spy just as I leaned into a fighting position. The spy jumped out of the way, using an elegant cartwheel.

I was expecting something of the sort and executed a whirling jump to land in the proximity of the spy. A small glow began to grow in the hand of the spy. I moved fast and struck her in the chest with a sidekick. The magic glow vanished as the dark figure rebounded from the blow in a backwards handspring.

This time the figure was ready for my attack and she leapt to meet me half way. Had anyone been in a position to see the fight that ensued, that person would have been witness to an excellent example of a duel between two very well-trained fighters, if I do say so myself. I had brought the confrontation down to hand-to-hand combat for two reasons. One, I was one of the best combat fighters in my field. Two, I hadn't a chance to gauge my opponent's magical skill. This was not the ideal situation to find that I was dealing with a powerful novice or a skilled coward. I knew she couldn't be an accomplished mage. She was doing someone else's dirty work.

As we faced each other for another series of blows and kicks, I found myself reveling in the adrenaline. This is what I had been craving for these long weeks during my undercover work. I loved the action and reaction of a good fight. The instantaneous and breathless decisions and actions. This is why I had joined up with the service, not that there had ever been a question about it.

However much I enjoyed the fight, I knew I was going to have to take my opponent down soon. We had been too long on the roof and by this time someone was bound to be wondering what all the scuffling was about.

As the dark figure kicked out at me from low to the ground, I jumped into the air, somersaulting over my opponent. As I landed, I turned. My opponent, expecting a kick or a punch, leaned in and to the side of me. Exactly as I had planned it. I took a firm grip above my opponent's elbow, which I found surprisingly thin and easy to grasp. I turned her to face me. Our fight was now a wrestling match. I had five inches and 30 pounds on my opponent. As we locked into a pushing war that would have been the envy of any sumo wrestler, I smiled at the smaller figure.

In the blink of an eye it was all over. Summoning the direction with my breath, I took a step towards my opponent and twisted to the side sending my foe off balance. Without losing hold of the dark figure, I took the leap to headquarters.

From the unevenly floored rooftop darkened by the night, suddenly we were in a well-lit windowless hall. The dark figure, still masked, immediately realized the trouble she was in and tried to roll away from me. Before she could wrench herself free, another woman ran forward and threw out a nearly invisible net. As the net floated down around the spy, it disappeared as it covered the dark figure.

The entrance hall attendant, a graying middle-aged woman with round cheeks and short legs, began reading a typed up speech to the silent figure hugging her knees on the floor. "I hereby notify you that your magic has been bound by the powers invested in me, Agent Harker, of the American Mage Intelligence Service. You will be bound until further investigation of the committee looking into illegal entry into the American Mage Intelligence Service headquarters." The woman swirled her finger around in the air to indicate the building we were in.

When the attendant was finished, I reached over and pulled off the mask of my opponent. Sullenly sitting before me was a small woman with short dark hair. Her bright black eyes were set off by wide cheekbones and a fine mouth. While of Asian descent, she was not Chinese.

I eyed her intensely. "Interesting," I said more to myself than to the other agent. I looked at the other woman and smiled brightly. "Thanks Hennie, I was hoping you would be on duty."

"Any time Esme," Hennie said with a wink. I made to protest the shortened version of my name, but she said first, "I know, I know, I'm not supposed to call you that any more, Esmeralda. Its hard to get out of a habit of a lifetime you know." I rolled my eyes at yet another reminder that to most of the agents, I would always be a child. Both Hennie and I looked down at our captive. "I see you haven't lost your touch for trouble."

"You know me Hennie, trouble always just seems to turn up."

Chapter 2

Ocean Paradise Resort, Jamaica

June 17, 1959

I spread myself out on a lounge chair to soak up the morning sun. The ocean waves lightly splashing against the shore next to me. I put on my sunglasses and leaned my head against the pillow. This was just what I needed to unwind. The hot sun, the salt air and stiff drink at my side. After the verbal lashing I had received from Mistress, I definitely needed a vacation, even if it was a forced leave of absence. Although, between me and my diary, it wasn't so forced.

I had spent the last three months going from one assignment to another. With all the spy networks lighting up like Christmas trees lately, something big was going down. I sipped my frozen daiquiri. It wasn't my job to save the world and it wasn't my fault that the Beijing job got blown out, I thought to myself. Although, deep down I knew I had blown my own cover.

I was on two weeks forced leave and spending my second day at the Ocean Paradise Resort in Jamaica. I had pooled much of my savings for an extravagant week at this posh resort and I meant to enjoy every last bit of sunlight. I had spent the first few days of my leave punching up my wardrobe. Most of my clothes, at least my very nice pieces, were horribly out of fashion. It had taken my several trips to the sundry store and hours managing a needle and thread, but I was satisfied that I would appear, if not at the height of fashion, then at least admirably fashionable.

The sun radiated down into my skin and I could feel my muscles relaxing. Even my magic, that tiny bit of vibration that was always with me but not part of me, evened out into a low tingly buzz.

The waiter came to replace my drink and I noticed with half-open eyes that he looked appreciatively at my bikini-clad body. I was under no pretensions that I was a beauty, but I enjoyed the appreciative looks. In my own way, I was quite pretty and given the chance to show off my charm, magical or otherwise, I could be very attractive.

I smiled to myself as I thought of the night before. Almost as soon as I had arrived at the hotel bar, looking ravishing in a light pink dinner dress, I had been approached by Jerry, a swarthy Cuban. Jerry had flirted relentlessly with me the whole evening and I had eaten it up. Jerry was what one might call a professional gigolo. No need for a truth spell to see through that guy. Jerry on the other hand could have used a truth spell, quite a strong one too, for he was under the impression that I was married to a French count who didn't like the sun.

"Jerry was fun," I said quietly to myself, "But I hope he lays off tonight. I think I'd like a bit of romance that isn't so mercenary." I gave a great big stretch and was about to turn over when my heard a quiet tick tick ticking coming from my handbag. I leaned over and looked inside my bag. I knew it. My compact was going off. I reached for it reflexively, but stopped before my hand touched it.

"Dammit," I pulled my hand back. Closing my bag, I tossed it into the sand away from me. Mistress was trying to contact me again. My compact had gone off the night before too, just when Jerry was getting nice and appreciative of my 'golden brown hair and liquid eyes'. I had ignored it then as well, but the ticking got so loud and annoying that even Jerry interrupted his well-rehearsed flirtation in confusion at the source of the noise.

I turned over in growing frustration. The ticking noise steadily beat away. Just when I'm getting nice and relaxed, I thought. Barely containing a sharp 'harumph' I closed I eyes. The warm sun felt heavenly on my back. I tried to let all my work hassles go, to concentrate only on the sound of the nearby waves.

It was no good. I couldn't stop my mind from going over and over again the scene in Mistress's office after the Beijing debacle.

After Hennie had taken the prisoner to the keep, I had gone to the showers. I returned that awful orange robe to wherever it came from, even though I thought I might be doing the owner a favor by getting rid of it altogether. After showering off, I summoned some of my own clothes from my apartment in New York, along with the fading glamour, then went to meet my destiny in the office of Mistress Parks.

I had known Mistress since I was born. Even then, Mistress had been head of the Mage Intelligence Service. Mistress had long known my mother and had worked with my grandmother at one time. I had once mouthed off to Mistress and referred to her early years as "before recorded time." She hadn't denied it. Mistress was a very old woman. So old she seemed to beyond counting her age in years. My mother, Brigitta, had told me that she had even seemed that old even when she had been a girl.

There I was walking into Mistress's office, full of grand old furniture, for another berating for messing up. I was glad I hadn't ever begun counting how many times I'd been to the old woman's office after getting in trouble. Even then, after more than twelve years as an agent for AMIS, what we called the American Mage Intelligence Service for short, I felt like a 10 year-old in trouble for turning my instructor blue.

At the door to the office, I paused. Gripping the filmy, unsubstantial glamour, I let out a large sigh then knocked using the large brass lions' head knocker. At once the door unlatched and I pushed my way through it.

Mistress sat behind a huge ornately carved oak desk. The shriveled old woman looked child-sized in comparison to her desk. Her white hair pulled back into a neat bun, her wool suit impeccable, her wizened eyes pale and piercing, her gnarled hands tightly folded before her on the green blotter created a rather foreboding image. It was a scene that I had encountered hundreds of times before. Now it barely even caught my attention.

"Esmeralda O'Rourke." Mistress stated flatly.

"Yes Mistress."

"Would you care to report on your botched undercover assignment?" There was no change in her voice. I remained silent. I knew it was no use getting baited into speaking. Mistress knew what happened already. I would wait until she asked specific questions. After years of facing Mistress and falling into the traps she set out so you could hang yourself, I discovered that the less I said the better I could mitigate my punishments.

"I had planned for you to stay there at least through the month." Mistress paused and raised a wrinkly eyebrow, "You are fortunate that you obtained a small amount of good information before you were . . . caught out."

Still I held my tongue. Now Mistress was practically taunting me. It was so unfair. Mistress paused while she scrutinized me. I thought of cocktails on the beach at sunset.

"The agent you caught, whoever she is, was carrying a jinx. When Hennie bound her magic it also bound her tongue. We'll get nothing out of her," Mistress said levelly, "But, she will no longer be a threat."

The espionage of magic can at times be a war of attrition. There are only so many magic workers in the world and even fewer who can use their powers in such a way as to be an effective operative. Mistress and I both knew that whoever the trapped witch was, she had been very well trained and a key operative.

"Tell me Esmeralda, who do you think she worked for?"

I relaxed a tiny bit. The worst part was over. "The Chinese service or Arcanimus, ma'am," was my curt response.

"And pray tell why?"

"Those are the two entities that would want to monitor activity in regards to magical weapons."

"Are you certain? Perhaps a third party didn't want the U.S. to get that information. Certainly you see what I mean?" Mistress asked using her sweet old lady voice. I was having nothing of it.

"Yes, ma'am, that is definitely a factor. However, it seems to me that a third party would have tried to take me out of the picture. This operative merely confirmed my identity before running."

"Very good Esmeralda. Now who would have the most to lose by the information of the weapons sale?"

"The Arcanimus, ma'am. As they operate in total secrecy, they wouldn't want any other agency outside of China knowing about the deal."

"Now, dear, I am looking into a number of factors relating to your . . . inconclusive assignment. You, however, will be taking a two week leave of absence. Please use the time wisely to reflect on your most recent assignment and how it could have been performed with greater . . . tact."

Mistress nodded indicating that I was free to go.

My compact was ticking fiercely. It probably sounded like a bomb. I squeezed my eyes shut and concentrated on relaxing, but it was no good.

"Mistress probably just wants to rub it in that I failed in my assignment," I muttered, pushing myself up into a sitting position. I gulped down my daiquiri and grabbed my towel. As I walked down to the water, I had to hold my head, having induced a freezing spike headache from drinking the daiquiri too fast.

I dropped the towel just above the tide line and walked out into the warm Caribbean waters. Swimming would make me feel better. Exercise was just the thing to clear my mind. Once up to my waist in the shallow waves I dived forward, relishing the cool water around me. A few yards into my swim, I absent-mindedly thought to myself for perhaps the five thousandth time, "If only mom was here."

And that was it. I knew that clearing my mind was out of the question. I swam on.

My mother, the famous opera singer Birgitta O'Rourke, had been missing for nearly seven years. Like me, my mother was a member of the Service. When she went missing, she wasn't on assignment. She was in Rome, singing the part of Isolde at La Scala. Then she was gone. I didn't know if she was alive or dead, but as the years passed it seemed more and more likely that she wasn't holed up waiting for a storm to blow over.

Birgitta had been Mistress's right-hand woman since she joined the service the year she turned 18. Mistress in the early years had been a comrade to my grandmother, Siobhan. Siobhan O'Rourke was a senior member of the Irish department of the British Royal Order of Magicial Service at the turn of the century. She couldn't abide the British and when she was offered citizenship in the United States, she took it eagerly. I never met my grandmother, by all accounts an exceptional sorceress. She had died in the line of duty long before I was born. Just like her mother before her, my mother was born to be in the Service, but she had another calling as well.

As it turned out being an international opera star was the perfect cover for a AMIS agent. One of Mother's best talents was her ability to teleport. She was a master at it. She could jump to a place she had only heard about. Most agents, most magical people in fact, couldn't jump to any place they had never physically been to before. I wasn't nearly the jumper that my mother was, but I wasn't so bad either.

It wasn't as if I saw my mother all that much before her disappearance, but she was always just a jump away if I needed her. And if felt that I needed her more the older I got.

I had reached the floating platform 50 yards out from the beach. I pulled myself up onto the wooden deck that smelled of salt water and warmed wood. My mind was no clearer, but the tension was gone. In its place was the terrible ache I got in my chest when I allowed myself to miss my mother. I lay down flat on the planks and felt the sunshine beat down on my wet skin. Lazily I stretched, putting my arms over my head, and gave a great sigh. I heard waves hitting the side of the platform, but I didn't bother to look for its cause.

I did notice when the platform shifted suddenly as if it had been slammed into. Jerking up to a sitting position, I saw a 40-foot yacht just ocean-side of the platform. I put a hand up to shield my eyes for a better view. On the bow of the ship, not ten feet from me, was a man dressed in a finely tailored boating suit. His handsome tan face was smiling broadly.

"You must be quite a swimmer, young lady, to make it out here."

I smiled back. Things were certainly looking up. Immediately I pictured in my mind a quiet, romantic dinner on board the yacht, this stranger's handsome face across the table from me.

"It's not that far, really," I got up and moved closer to the yacht so that the sun would be out of my eyes.

"Enjoying your holiday?" The stranger said convivially. He had a slight accent, not quite British, not quite French.

"Very much," I replied with a flirtatious smile. "Are you on holiday as well, or is it your business to sail around the Caribbean on a beautiful boat?"

As I spoke the handsome stranger bounded over the edge of the ship, landing squarely on the platform. Better and better, I thought.

"I generally conduct my business while sailing around the Caribbean. Today, I believe I'll take a break."

"It's important for one to have some relaxation. No one wants to be a dull boy after all."

"Perhaps I could persuade you to join me for a tour of the coast this afternoon?"

"I would..." just then I felt as if someone was tugging at my intestines. Silently I cursed Mistress, for I knew exactly what that feeling meant.

Across from me the stranger looked confused. He shook his head slightly as if to refocus his eyes. When I had felt the tug, the poor man had momentarily had double vision as a piece of me was tugged away from my body. I felt sorry for the man, for he was probably thinking he was seeing things.

During the war, when Mother was on long-term assignment in Europe, Mistress had become my guardian. About the same time, my abilities had begun to manifest rapidly. I thought it very funny to pop off to Singapore for noodles or to Argentina for empanadas or even to Australia for an afternoon on the beach. It drove Mistress to distraction that I would never stay put. She really did have enough to worry about with a war going on. So, when I was about 10, Mistress had spelled a fail-safe tracking system on me. When Mistress wanted me to come, all she had to do was say the incantation and instantly I would be yanked back to headquarters. Mistress, finding the spell useful, especially with me, had never removed it. The tug that I felt that morning in Jamaica was Mistress's way of telling me that if I didn't pick up my compact soon, I would be yanked back under duress.

"I would love to," I continued after a slight hesitation, "but I have some business of my own to attend to this afternoon."

"Ah, well then, another time," the stranger responded, his eyes crinkling in his tan face. "But before we part, allow me to introduce myself. My name is Jacques Quincompoix." He finished with a slight bow.

"Mine is Esmeralda O'Rourke. Hopefully we will run into each other again soon." We both reached out to shake hands, but Jacques gallantly leaned over and kissed mine. With a leap of considerable athletic skill, Jacques climbed aboard his ship and waved farewell. I waved back and then dived in the water.

"Just as things were getting interesting," I thought as I stroked towards the shore, "Mistress has to get tough on me. I'm on mandatory leave for heavens sake." Similar petulant thoughts raced through my head as I reached the shore, toweled off, and walked back to my lounge chair.

I grabbed my bag from the spot where my left it and pulled out my compact. I opened it and held it up, running my fingers through my wet hair.

"Yes?" my spoke quietly to the tiny, round mirror.

"It's about time you checked in," came Mistress's harsh voice, now made tinny from the way it was amplified through the mirror.

I didn't say a word. I ran a finger under my lip as if I were correcting my lipstick. Just a precaution in case anybody happened to be looking my way. Mistress, her small reflection glowering, waited for a reply. When she received none, she continued.

"You are needed at headquarters at once. I expect you in the next 20 minutes."

"I'll be there in an hour. I need to check out of the hotel, don't I."

Mistress's lips grew tight together at my cheeky response, but she agreed. "Yes, its best if you consider your vacation over."

I snapped shut the compact and in a huff, grabbed for my bag and beach robe. In 40 minutes I had packed, checked out of the hotel–giving the excuse that unexpected family business had come up–and was in a taxi on the way to the airport. It was much easier to make a leap from a busy airport. No one took much notice of anyone else. Once inside the airport, I went to the women's restroom and simply took the jump from there.

I landed in my designated spot in the "entrance hall" of AMIS headquarters. The subterranean offices of the Service were located far underneath Washington, D.C.

In the entrance hall, around the walls there were name plates. On the floor before these were squares marked off on the floor. Each member of the AMIS had their own place in which to materialize. It was quite an honor the day you got your official spot. Plus it cut down on the interconnected spells that could occur should two people teleport to the same spot at the same time. That got messy.

I waved hello to the on-duty entrance monitor, a new recruit named Evelyn, and walked the length of the grand entrance hall towards the offices, glancing involuntarily at my own mother's nameplate.

At the door to Mistress's office, I knocked loud and impetuously, then opened the door.

"Trying to make a grand entrance, dear?" Mistress asked without looking up from the pile of papers she was perusing.

"I am reporting as requested, ma'am," was my curt reply. I stood at attention before Mistress's grand desk, hands tucked behind me.

"I see that. I must add that its about time as you were wanted yesterday evening for debriefing." Mistress fell silent for a time while she continued her paperwork. "However, you are here now and we'll have to do what we can."

"You received a message from your informant, Peter Masaryk. You are to meet him today. All the usual circumstances apply."

"Yes, ma'am," responded I automatically, but a shadow of worry crossed my face.

"Why does this message worry you?" asked Mistress, missing nothing. She looked up at me.

"It's nothing really. Peter told me that he wouldn't be contacting me any longer, since he was promoted, unless it was very important."

"I see," said Mistress, looking back down at my papers. "I am very curious to find what information Peter has for us. I have received reports from every continent that the Arcanimus are planning something very large, yet no one has any specifics."

"Yes, ma'am," I could barely keep the boredom out of my voice. If my had a dollar for every time I had heard that "the Arcanimus were planning something" I'd be rich, I was sure.

"I know you've heard that one before, dear. However, recent events and reports indicate that ever since Himiko has usurped governing power over the group, more sinister plots have been undertaken. Find out what you can from Peter. If it is as you say, he may have the key information that we've been missing."

"Yes ma'am."

"I won't be available after 4 o'clock today, so please report to me first thing tomorrow morning. I'll let you go now to prepare for your rendezvous." Mistress lifted her hand in a half wave, still holding a pen. I turned and left.

It was not quite noon East Coast time. That only gave me an hour to get myself in place. I rushed down the hall to my spot in the entrance hall and took off without another word to anybody.

Chapter 3

Prague

June 17, 1959

Mist was rising off of the river Vltava. I leaned against the balustrade on the North side of the Charles Bridge in Prague, dangling a hand bag over the river. The bridge was nearly deserted. The sun had just dipped behind the buildings and the only other people on the bridge seemed eager to cross it.

I was wearing a glamour of a poor old woman, dressed in a baggy dress with a coat many times patched. I stared unwaveringly at the river, as if I were contemplating its source. I huddled close to the statue of St. Anne. Any passerby who took any notice of me at all would think that I was homeless and would then do their best to ignore me completely.

That was just the way I wanted it. The Charles Bridge was the usual spot where I met my informant. Peter had once been an informant for my mother as well, but in those days the rendevous point had been near to the statue of St. Christopher. The bridge was a perfect spot to meet, as Peter crossed it every morning and evening on his way to and from his job in the Old Town. He had been a reliable source of information for many years. I considered him quite an old friend. I had first met him when I was very young, before the war, when I had accompanied my mother on a routine meeting with him.

The night's rendevous would be slightly more dangerous than that first time. Peter worked for the historical museum of Prague that also doubled as headquarters for the Czech network. With his democratic sympathies and his knowledge of magic espionage – his mother had worked for the Austrian Empire's network – he made a perfectly placed informant. In recent years as he climbed the managerial ranks, his information became more thorough and accurate, but the risks were greater. I knew that he had just recently been promoted to Assistant Director of the Cultural Museum.

Perfectly confident in Peter's abilities, I continued staring out over the darkening river. Peter was very late, but that didn't mean too much. At least, I shouldn't read too much into it. At thirty minutes past seven, I did allow herself to become a bit anxious. Our original meeting time was ten minutes past seven—Peter's usual time to pass over the bridge after he left the museum. Twenty minutes late was too much time. It would mean Peter was tremendously off his normal schedule. I risked a look around, but the bridge was quiet. I took a deep breath and forced myself to stare straight ahead. Everything would be fine, I told myself over and over again.

At nearly 7:40 I heard footsteps approaching from the Old Town side of the bridge. Holding my breath and concentrating, I listened closely to hear if the steps started to slow as they neared my position on the bridge. They did. I let out my breath quietly and mentally prepared myself for the meeting. German, we would be talking in German. Just then a tall, lean man with a weak chin and bright eyes, leaned against the wall about four feet away. I glanced up as if his presence meant nothing to me.

"Good evening ma'am," the middle-aged man began congenially. He casually pulled out a pack of cigarettes and prepared to light one. "If you let your bag hang over the edge like that, you will surely lose it."

Without turning to him, I replied, "If I leave it by my side a thief such as yourself might take it."

Out of the corner of my eye I could see the man grin at me. He lit the cigarette and drew in a deep breath. As he blew out the smoke, in a hushed voice he continued, "I'm delighted to see you my dear, but tonight is too risky."

As he spoke footsteps sounded on the pavement nearby. Two or three sets of footsteps all moving too quickly to be normal. I steeled myself for action, every nerve and muscle poised to move at a moment's notice.

Peter crumpled up the cigarette pack in his hand. "Take the trash and go. Don't you dare follow me." As he moved away from the balustrade, he tossed the crumpled cigarette pack over his shoulder towards the river.

"To me!" I willed silently and opened my hand inconspicuously to receive the small ball of paper. Once it was safely in my hand I turned towards the retreating Peter. Shaking a fist at his back I called out in a cackly voice in perfect, unrefined Czech, "Don't litter in my river you dirty scoundrel. Ruining the only thing left that is beloved to me."

I wailed like a crazy woman until I was roughly grabbed by the arm and swung around. I faced a tall man who could have been Arab except for his height and his light hair and eyes. In German he shouted at me and pointed at the retreating man. I understood him perfectly, but pretended I could not. Two other men hurried past him in pursuit of Peter. I pulled and tugged at the strong grasp of the one who held me, shouting profanities in Czech and accusing him of being a coconspirator in the littering scheme. Finally the unusual looking man threw me down and stormed off after his fellows.

Continuing to scream curses at the retreating men, I hauled myself up to my feet. I gradually toned down the curses until I was whispering and then I stopped completely. My eyes were fixed on the other side of the bridge. Peter and his pursuers were no longer visible.

Standing near the balustrade, I pocketed the ball of paper from Peter. I then closed my eyes in concentration and folded my hands together. In a second I leaned back onto the balustrade as my glamour took a step away from me. I watched as the old woman I had pretended to be slump off while muttering to herself. At the end of the bridge, about 30 feet away, it turned the corner and disappeared.

Now in no disguise but my own face and clothes, I hurried in the opposite direction to catch up with Peter and his pursuers. I didn't stand out much more than I had as the poor old woman other than I was dressed more fashionably and better than was often seen in post-war communist Prague.

Shouldering my bag and lowering my head, I rushed across the bridge, as if I were late for an appointment. I had last seen Peter's pursuers turn into an alleyway about a block past the end of the bridge. Not running, but walking with the longest strides I could muster, I had reached the alley in short order.

Without hesitation I turned down the dark corridor. Night had fallen heavily over the city and the alley was unlit by street lamps. I was equal to the darkness. I walked with purpose, holding tightly to my bag and cupping a shield spell in my hand near my heart.

I could hear moving things along the narrow path and passed shut doors illuminated by cracks of light. I saw nothing of the men I was after. The alley ended at the next street. The bright lights of the cars and cafes ruined my night vision and made me look away. Just then a bright flash of light caught my eye, coming from a dark space between buildings about twenty feet to my right.

It could have been just a camera flash, but I knew that no camera flash, however technologically advanced, would flash purple. That was the flash of a powerful spell. I took off at a run. Just as I got to the walkway between two large old buildings I slowed. Cautiously I peered around the corner. Fifteen feet away the walkway ended, the exit barred by an ornate iron gate. Backlit by the light in the courtyard beyond the gate, I could see three men moving over something immobile on the ground.

I stepped into the darkness of the walkway. Winding my arm like a softball pitcher, I lobbed a little spark towards the men at the far end. In a second, a bright light flared at the top of the covered walkway. In unison the three faces of the men pursuing Peter turned towards me. Each then put a hand up to shade their eyes from the light as they peered towards the street, vainly trying to make out the source of the magic.

Before any of the kneeling men could react, I had used Witness on the scene. The immobile object lying beneath the men at the far end of the walkway was Peter. Peter's body rested in a position that no living human could have borne, unconscious or awake. Peter was dead.

I began to cry out in shock and without a moment's wavering I made the leap to my own apartment in New York. Whether or not my neighbor's were startled by a sudden, piercing scream that afternoon, I didn't bother to know.

In the bright afternoon sunlight and in the comfort of my own home, I collapsed to the floor in tears. Peter had been a pillar to me. Even before I had become a full-fledged agent, he had helped me through a number of scrapes. He was my safety net in the Eastern block and in just a split second he was gone. The golden color of the afternoon sun streaming through my windows was a stark contrast to the damp, dark streets I had left moments before.

Remembering my duty and knowing that in my pocket I held the clues I needed to find his killers, I came back to my senses. I washed my face and straightened myself up. When I felt that I had pulled myself together, I took a deep breath and made the jump to headquarters. It was only 2:15 east coast time, and Mistress would need to know about Peter immediately.

Evelyn was still on duty. She leaned over a magazine on the desk before her. As I appeared, Evelyn looked up with a warm, welcoming smile on my face. As soon as she saw my haggard face, her smile dropped.

"Tell Mistress I'm coming to see her now. Its urgent." I turned on my heel and walked at a quick clip the length of the entrance hall. No longer did I have time for enthusiastic hellos. I could hear Evelyn on the office communicator announcing me to Mistress.

This time I didn't bother to knock at the door to Mistress's office. Mistress was looking into the oval mirror that stood on the bureau behind her desk. Upon my entrance, she held up a hand to silence me.

Nodding into the mirror, Mistress said softly, "Yes, I see. Uh-hum, yes, certainly. I'll be in contact when I have information." Mistress folded the mirror down into its case then turned to face me.

"I believe you have terrible news."

"Yes ma'am."

"Have a seat and let me hear it," Mistress said indicating the leather upholstered chair before her desk.

I did as I was told. Very professionally I gave Mistress all the details of what I had witnessed. If I felt the tears stinging my eyes again, no one would have known it. I did brush my hair away from my face more than necessary. Mistress remained silent throughout and my recital was soon over.

"Let's see what you got with Witness," was the only response Mistress gave. She pushed a button on the panel next to the phone on her right-hand side. A small projector-like apparatus reveled itself on the edge of the desk. It pointed at the empty wall to the left.

I pulled Witness from my pocket and gripped the small, flat disk in my hand. It looked like a thin piece of round glass, no more than 2 inches in diameter, a lense from a pair of glasses. On its own it really was just a piece of opaque glass, but in the hands of a capable agent, it acted as a secondary memory. Witness was a memory without the ego or interpretation that is a person's actual memory and it was a very handy field tool.

I slipped the thin glass circle into the fitted slot on the projector. With a wave of my hand over the apparatus, a light appeared on the empty wall. It took a few moments for Witness to focus on the recently recorded scene in Prague. Mistress nodded approvingly as the picture became clearer. It only lasted a few seconds before it went blank.

Mistress waved her own hand over the projector, playing the image backwards. Then she made it stop. We were both silent as we closely examined the image. Clearly it showed the faces of two women and one man. Another useful aspect of Witness, often it saw through loosely bound glamours. I had been sure it was three men that had followed Peter.

"Do you recognize any one of those people?" Mistress asked.

I shook my head no. "I do," replied Mistress. "The woman on the far right is a discredited Turkish agent." The woman Mistress spoke of was clearly much older than her two companions. The white in her short, graying hair caught the light exceptionally well, showing off a wrinkled forehead and well-lined eyes. "I haven't heard a word of her since before the war ended. It would make sense of course if she were now involved with the Arcanimus."

I studied the faces on the wall, memorizing them, searching my own true memories for some key to Peter's murder.

"Now, let's see this cigarette pack that Peter gave you." She pressed the same button on her control panel and the projector faded. A light tinkling noise was made as my witness rattled onto the desk. I pulled out the balled up pack and smoothed it out on Mistress's desk between us.

The packet had been torn open and on the inside was writing. It looked like a list, handwritten in haste.

> *Arcn*
>
> *Iris prj.*
>
> *perrin*
>
> *lamscus*
>
> *cosat*
>
> *jul *

We studied the paper, both craning our necks so we each could read it. The first three items were easily deduced. Arcn. must mean the Arcanimus. I didn't know what the Iris Project was, but at least it was legible. Perrin, of course, referred to Dr. Amelda Perrin, the eminent French researcher of the arcane. The last three items were not so clear. "jul \\" could be a date. Although, with "cosat" or "lamscus" it could be a phrase or part of a sentence that tied the first three items together.

Having memorized the message, I looked at Mistress expectantly. I was certain Mistress would know what was going on.

Mistress wore a look of deep concern. Between her dusty gray eyebrows were two thick worry lines. She held a finger to her lips, concentrating.

"My dear, what do you make of this message?"

I stifled a sigh. I wished, just for once, that Mistress would speak before asking a question. Still the mystery at hand was more important than conquering the conversation, so I answered.

"Arcanimus, Iris Project, Dr. Perrin, a couple of unintelligible items and maybe a date—July?"

"Yes, that is exactly what I think too," Mistress answered hesitantly. "I have heard the term Iris Project from several different sources recently, but have yet to determine its scope. I know for a fact that it is related to some new plot put forth by those fools in the Arcanimus. However, I have no idea what fourth and fifth items mean. As today is June 17th, that doesn't give us much time before July to figure this out."

"Unless it is a date late in July," I pointed out. Mistress gave my a look that clearly indicated that I should keep my mouth closed for the present.

Mistress looked up at the clock. It was already 3:15 p.m. "I will send the cigarette pack paper to the FBI for a handwriting analysis. We'll want to make sure that it is Peter's writing. With the proper comparisons, the analysts should be able to determine the true letters of the last two items on the list. It is obvious that Peter was in too much haste to write properly."

"I haven't heard a word of Dr. Perrin since the International Coven last fall," she continued. "I'll contact the Legation Francois immediately. Esmeralda, I'll need you on call for the time being. You will be going to visit Dr. Perrin as soon as the legal channels are cleared and she agrees to receive you."

I nodded. I had expected as much.

"You can go now, but please keep your compact handy. You will be needed." Mistress turned again to the bureau behind her desk. She raised the oval mirror from its box. I didn't wait to see who she was contacting.

Once outside the office, I leaned against the wall and let out a long breath. What a day it had been. Was it just five hours before that I had been sunning myself in Jamaica?

Chapter 4

New York City

June 18, 1959

When I had left Mistress's office, my intention had been to go straight home and get to sleep. I wanted to be well rested for whatever was going to come next. But I was far too restless to sleep and as it was still quite early, I went out for some dinner and then to the movies. Unfortunately the film that was playing was one of those film noirs, all dark alleyways and shady characters. The scenery was far too similar to where I had just been and the movie did nothing to distract me from poor Peter's murder.

I went home then and tried to sleep, but it was long in coming and short in duration. Magic was building in me in answer to my restlessness. The anticipation I felt for my next assignment had my body collecting and storing magic which just served to make me more restless. Before dawn I was up. I went through my callisthenics routine and then headed out for a walk.

I thought about jumping back to headquarters to get out my extra energy by some sparring practice or by leading a training session with some of the newer recruits, but I couldn't face anyone right then. I chose to walk alone.

I headed towards Battery Park. It was near to the longest day of the year and the sun was already coming out, long before the city was starting to wake. It was a long walk, but it felt good to move. I walked fast and thought a lot.

As I reached the park, the sun had just fully risen across the river. The water glinted as if it were on fire and as no one else was nearby, I risked throwing a few lightening balls into the sea after humming a quick incantation to divert attention from myself. I found myself much calmer after the long walk and target practice. It was going to be a very hot, humid day, but as the sun rose higher, it warmed me in a good way.

A half an hour later there were people out on the streets, beginning their days. A street vendor came around and I bought coffee and a danish. At the ferry terminal to the Statue of Liberty, I saw a large group of tourists arrive and decided to join them. Like all witches, I didn't much like being in a boat. Our connection to magic became scattered and unpredictable over water. That's why during any witch trial, the accusers would dunk the supposed witch in water.

I paid for my ferry ticket and got on. I went to the bow and leaned against the rail. The sea breeze felt wonderful on my face, but the fizzling of my magic connection was somewhat worrisome. I didn't think too much about it. Mistress could still reach me by mirror and the ride was only 20 minutes long.

Watching the early morning sea made me maudlin. I couldn't stop picturing the flash of purple light that must have killed Peter. For all my training–the years of wrestling and gymnastics training, my studies both esoteric and mundane, being tutored by my mother and Mistress (both magical geniuses)–seemed to be for nothing if I could not save a friend.

If he had only said something, I could have teleported him from St. Charles bridge in two seconds and he would have been safe. I had first jumped with him when I was only 8. My mother had a lunch appointment with him and she had sent me to take him to her favorite restaurant in Paris. Even then he had trusted my skills. Why not yesterday?

But I knew the answer to that. Peter was not magical. He had spent his whole life studying the history of Czechoslovakia and had worked his way up the staff at the historical museum. His life's work was the history of his country, but if I had jumped with him from the bridge, his secrets would have been wide open. He would have been caught out as a spy. It didn't matter that he never handed over to me secrets of the state. At the very least he would have lost his position. He would likely have been arrested by the Communists government and imprisoned, if not tortured.

He chose his own death, I think. Yet, it didn't make me feel any better that I had let him die.

His death would be put down as a random crime. His sisters, both fine folk witches, would know what happened. They would arrange his funeral.

Sometimes it seemed very unfair to me that men did not have much of a share in magic. Granted, it was one of the few things women held over men, if only the world had a better knowledge of it.

People have always known that there are some of us who can control the magic in this world. I think everyone senses that the magic is there—at least from my scanty experience out in the world among regular people. I don't pretend to know much about how regular people live. It's not my job, nor my area of interest.

In previous times, witches, magical people were revered in many cultures. Brought up to serve kings and emperors. The Oracle of Delphi, so very famous everywhere, was really a nunnery for witches who declined to participate in any one court or government. The Hsu Shi, in ancient China, were the elite scholars of the emperor's court. All were women, but raised as men. They even took wives and were held in very high esteem. In Russia, for centuries, the Czarist court had practiced a form of eugenics in order to bring out the magic in men. The manly czars wouldn't hear of having women troops. It would never do to have a regiment of Baba Yaga's patrolling the Kremlin. The magic corps were the ideal military unit. All tall, strong and youthful soldiers who could wield some of the top magic.

The ferry boat docked at the Statue of Liberty and I followed the tourists off the boat. I had no intention of going up the statue, but instead wandered around the island grounds. I watched the city skyline for a long time, lost in thought, my mind skipping from one subject to the next.

Then there were the middle ages and reformation. Witches were not looked upon so kindly then. And that is exactly why most women able to use magic keep it to themselves. Many never even know they have that connection. On the whole, most witches have a very small magic. They can heal small wounds and sicknesses or cause minor harm. Perhaps move from one place to another quicker than they ought to be able to–a precursor to teleporting. They can turn only a few people's thoughts at a time. That's why persecuted witches couldn't escape a mob.

In rural places where people live in small villages, it makes sense to keep magic to yourself. Help your fellow villagers where you can, but keep it small and keep it to yourself. Silence about magic has never been mandatory or legislated, but every witch instinctively knows to keep quiet about it.

Yet it never stopped governments from wanting to use that magic themselves. By the 18th century all western governments had an organized unit of witches at their disposal. One of the first thing the founding fathers of the United States did was organize a group of witches to be at the disposal of George Washington's army. Those women have gone down in history as washer women moonlighting as nurses that followed the Continental Army. Most of the volunteers in the revolution were not very powerful mages, but they helped at crucial points in the war of Independence.

I think that several centuries ago some powerful, but benign, witch figured out that the best way from keeping the powerful witches from trying to take over the world was to put them to use taking care of the world, by supporting their countries however they could.

Early on witches were an integral part of decision making on the part of governments, especially in Britain and France during the height of each country's imperialism. Every king, queen, or minister had their own personal witch. Now we are relegated to the field of espionage and cover-up. In our department of the dozen or so active field agents we have four talented witches who are experts at misdirection and memory removal. They are the busiest office we have.

I would love to be as busy as they are, but I could never spend my days doing the quiet work of Turned Thoughts. I would be horrible at it too. People should be allowed to think what they want to, do what they want, even if they see something they should not, even if they know something they should not.

That wouldn't do for me anyway. I'm from a long line of people who are doers. "What is bred in the bone" is not far from the truth for me. It's always been hard for me to sit still or wait. My job is perfect for me. Except for those days that I can't keep friends from being killed.

I have a very strong connection to the magic. I am one of the most powerful witches in AMIS, but I'm not the strongest. Yet, there are very few like me. It gets kind of lonely. I've never spent much time around regular people. My mother's opera company when I was very young, but hardly any people since.

When I first became a true agent at AMIS, I had a lot of down time and took some classes at community college. I made friends with several girls in my classes and for a time we would spend afternoons and weekends together. It was a fun time for me as those were the first friends I made that didn't know any-thing about me. I still keep in touch with them all these years later, Christmas cards and baby showers, but they've all moved on in their normal lives. A few are married with a number of small children. And two are career girls, an accountant and a clerk, who work nine to five jobs. In either case, I have noth-ing in common with them any more. They think I work as a stewardess and travel all the time. I can't really talk to them and if I were to feed them a story about my life, its just as if I were working undercover. There is no real connection to them. It's all a lie.

Sometimes I envy those friends—living their lives at the speed of time. Just like these tourists around me. They save their money and buy a plane ticket or a train ticket, they go and do their visiting, then go home and start over again. I wonder what that would be like?

Boring for me as I know there are other ways of moving about. Having to wait to save up to buy a ticket, or even sit on a train for hours on end would kill me. I sighed, leaning over the railing on the ferry.

When the ferry landed, I went back to the park and bought another cup of coffee. It was still early in the day and I didn't have anything to do but wait, so I took a seat on a bench with the old men reading newspapers and one old woman feeding the birds. So many other people came and went, so busy.

Most of my current friends, if you could call them that, were witches from other agencies in Western Europe, but as we all worked in the secret departments of our countries, we could only be so friendly. There was one woman who worked in our department who I was very friendly with, Lizzie. She worked for the accounting department. She had very little magic, but was a wiz at numbers. Due to the nature of my work, we rarely got to spend any time together. Even for her, working for AMIS, she still had a nine to five job.

I began missing my mother again. If she were here, I would never feel so lonely. Although I wouldn't be able to bear to tell her about Peter. They had been such close friends. Peter. I had promised myself that I wouldn't cry, and I hadn't, yet just then my eyes stung. Whether for Peter or my mother, I couldn't tell.

Those damn Arcanimus, I muttered aloud. No one noticed. The old man on the park bench across from me had been murmuring in his sleep for the past ten minutes and he was quite loud. The Arcanimus was probably why that benevolent witch so long ago figured out that to keep us out of trouble was to put us to work . . . against them.

The Arcanimus was an ancient society of witches. No one has produced an accurate history of their organization—sometimes a loose association, sometimes a well-trained, tight-knit magical force. Their first mention is around the first century BC. Like the witches at Delphi, the original Arcanimus group wanted nothing to do with regular people and their politics. Their intention had been to create a country of their own. It never happened. For centuries they have been plotting one scheme after another to try and control parts of the world or people themselves. Fortunately, most of those drawn to Arcanimus are more greedy and stupid and uncooperative with one another, than magically gifted. Their plotting has gained them no ground at all.

Yet now Himiko was their leader. If anyone could bully a group into a semblance of organization and give them the magic to support their plots, it was her. Maybe the most gifted witch this century, she had the bad luck to be raised at a bad time in history and raised by people who used and abused her great connection to magic.

I sighed wondering what Himiko would be like if she had been raised quietly and lovingly. The old man next to me had walked away leaving his newspaper. Tired of my own thoughts by this time, I picked up the paper. I scanned the headlines, but nothing caught my attention. Then, at the bottom of the front page, in a small-type headline, I saw a piece about an upcoming space launch from Cape Canaveral.

NASA LAUNCHING SELF-GENERATING COMMUNICATIONS SATELLITE

The launch date was July second.

Two items from Peter's hastily written note clicked into place. Co Sat was communications satellite. Jul ll was the second of July. I had to contact Mistress immediately.

I walked back to the railing that overlooked the bay. I took out my compact and quietly called to Mistress.

"Yes, yes what is it now?" I heard her tinny voice, but I couldn't see her face. Mistress was probably still facing her desk while answering her mirror.

"C-o-s-a-t means communications satellite. J-u-l-1-1 is July second. NASA's next big launch takes place then." I didn't see any reason for pleasantries or small talk.

Mistress's face came into view. "Yes," she began, a thoughtful expression on her face. "I believe you are on to something, my dear. But what? What are they planning to put up into empty space?"

"Whatever it is, that is what Project Iris is all about."

"I'm sure that is true. However, now that we know the date, we must discover what this Project Iris is."

"Anything from Dr. Perrin yet?" I asked hopefully.

"No, nothing yet. And those Legation witches are being most bureaucratic," Mistress replied, her nose lifting into the air. "Stay close to your mirror, dear. I believe I will be needing you soon."

"I'll be ready," I replied and shut the compact. With renewed purpose, I headed back to my apartment to make sure I was ready when the call to action came.

Chapter 5

Hermance, Geneva, the Swiss/French Border

June 20, 1959

Dawn was just beginning to break over the mountains in the east giving an eerie glow to the mist that hung low over the lake. Even though it was the middle of June, I was chilled through from the rarified air of the altitude. How people could choose to live in cold climates was beyond me. From the little I knew about my father, I knew that I got my distaste for cold from him.

I blew into my hands and rubbed them together. I was dressed as a summer tourist ready for a hike, and had I really been one, I would be in bed for a least another hour. If I had my way, I would be in bed for another seven hours since it was just midnight in New York. Yet duty called and I was there ready for action. Had I been any less confident, I would have been nervous of completing my new assignment, having botched two assignments in less than a week. But I could do this one. I knew it.

It was the third morning after Peter's death. I had spent the previous day fretting in my apartment waiting for the call to action from Mistress. It hadn't come until the evening. The Legation Francois had been unable to reach Dr. Perrin at her home laboratory or elsewhere. They wanted another day to try and locate her before AMIS got involved, but Mistress wouldn't hear of it and sent me on to try and locate the good doctor at her home on Lake Geneva.

I stifled a yawn and danced a quick jig for warmth. Golden light was spilling across the lake and I could hear people along the boulevard now. Once I had checked my watch to confirm the time, I left my waiting place and made for the boulevard, casting a wistful backward glance at the beautiful lake stretching out behind me.

With my backpack slung over my shoulder, I made for a nearby café for breakfast. Over steaming mugs of coffee and fresh croissant, I fell into a conversation in Italian and German with the shopkeeper. I was pretending to be an Italian health aficionado on holiday hiking the circuit of the lake. While I was fluent and accentless in both Italian and French, for the benefit of my disguise I pretended not to speak very good French.

At the end of my meal I got directions to a hiker's outfitter in order to get a new canteen. At this store, I made sure to speak to everyone I encountered in the shop. On the way out of the small town, I stopped by a delicatessen for a packed lunch. I told everyone how I was spending the whole day hiking to the village of Douvaine across the French frontier. A lot of pretense I know, yet I couldn't rule out spies. Dr. Perrin's property was very magically protected. Since we didn't know what her status was, Mistress had decided it was better if I hike in rather than just jumping to her property line. If there was a plot against Dr. Perrin, we couldn't be too careful.

Packed lunch safely stowed in my backpack, I set off to Dr. Perrin's house. The doctor lived on the Swiss-French border in a house her father had built for her in the 1920s. Clinging to a mountainside it was a marvel of architecture and from any of its windows there was an amazing view of Lake Geneva.

Dr. Amelda Perrin was the daughter of a Frenchman and a Moroccan witch. Her father was a wealthy colonialist who overturned custom by marrying his native concubine. Dr. Perrin was raised in Morocco and educated in France. Her father was unduly attached to his daughter and when her proclivity for research became evident, he arranged it so that she would never have to worry about money. He didn't want the whims of marriage to dictate how his beloved daughter lived her life.

Dr. Perrin was somewhat of a celebrity among those with magic. Her research between magic and science had informed many of the twentieth century's greatest developments. She was an odd woman, even for a magical adept, for she was extremely solitary and desired only her research—never the fame or fortune that came with mundane scientific research.

I had known her since the invasion of France in 1939. The Nazis had been trying to recruit Dr. Perrin to their team since the early 1930's. Hitler had assembled quite a group of magical adepts from all over Europe. Dr. Perrin would have been the lynch pin but she had no interest in international politics, let alone fascism. Even if she had political interests, as a French-Moroccan she would never have aligned herself with Germans.

After the fall of Paris, it became known that Hitler's team of witches, that operated under the thoughtful name of Schutz-staffel Frauen, or among the magic crowd, the SSF. The SSF were trying to develop a long-range broadcasting system. While Hitler was an entrancing speaker, his abilities were greatly enhanced by an amulet he wore that induced slight hypnotism. Schutzstaffel Frauen were working to be able to broadcast his speeches, along with the hypnotism capabilities, like a radio broadcast. Not coming up with anything themselves, they desperately needed Dr. Perrin.

Fortunately, when the Nazi's finally made their move and sent in an elite team of SSF operatives there were two legation members guarding the good Doctor. The Brits had a fabulous seer working with them during the war. She was quite accurate at predetermining events and locations, but was very vague on time specifics. She saw clearly that the Germans would make a kidnaping attempt on Dr. Perrin. The two legation agents barely got Dr. Perrin out of her house in time, one of them was critically wounded, and escorted her to Washington.

Dr. Perrin spent the remainder of the war years in a boring townhouse in Georgetown with a basement converted into a laboratory that contained any research material she might need.

That was when I got to know her. She didn't speak English, so didn't have much to do with the U.S. agents and witches—not that she ever spent much time with anybody. At that time, my mother was working deep undercover in Rome, and I was under Mistress's care. As I speak French, Mistress, trying to keep me out of trouble, gave me the task of being Dr. Perrin's secretary. Actually, I was more of a gopher—I brought her groceries, answered her mail, deflected anyone who wanted to see her.

Dr. Perrin was a surly middle-aged woman at that time. Yet for all her crankiness, she was always kind to me. She taught me a lot about magical research and more than a few useful spells. She may have grumbled a lot, but I think she deeply appreciated the care she was shown in the U.S. She was not ever comfortable being around people and I don't think she knew how to express her gratitude.

When the war was over and things were set right in France, many of the top witches in the world came together to lay protections over Dr. Perrin's property. She was much too valuable a resource to leave unprotected, or protected by any one nation. Dr. Perrin had been living in peace at her home since 1945. I just hoped things were still peaceful for her.

In a little over an hour, I had hiked the two and a half miles from Hermance to the turnoff I needed to take to Dr. Perrin's chateau. As close as it was to the French-Swiss boarder, a small dislocation spell had been used to blur the space. If you didn't know what you were looking for, you would walk right past it as if it wasn't there. No one without magic could tell you what country the property actually resided in. The house and its 15 acres of land always seemed to get lost on maps.

I had been with Mistress the day that Dr. Perrin's property had been removed from those maps. A large group of very powerful and influential witches had come together, each laying a spell on the property so that it would take someone, magical or otherwise, with a great deal of skill to sort through its defenses to find it. The resulting mixture of personal and group spells was extraordinary.

Even though I was just a teenager at the time, I had laid my own bit of magic on the property. It made me one of the few people in the world who could walk right up to the house. No one but the doctor herself could teleport in or out of the area, which was why I was going the old fashioned way, by foot.

Just as I was about to turn off the main road, I folded my hands and conjured up a bright flicker of light that rested just above my palm. It was a detection spell that told me if there was any living human within a quarter mile of me. The light glowed pale yellow, I was free and clear. I stepped on the path to Dr. Perrin's and, had there been anyone nearby to see, seemed to disappear into the folds of the protection spells.

It was another three quarters of a mile to the house itself. I enjoyed the walk. The day was clear and sunny, not yet too hot, and the scenery, of course, beautiful.

As I neared the bend in the track that led to the house, I stopped again to cast the detection spell. The light still flickered a pale yellow. There was no one in the Doctor's house. A chill ran down my spine as I made the connections. No one had heard from the doctor for some time and now I found her house to be unoccupied. That did not bode well.

I went more cautiously now, but still held a small bit of hope that Dr. Perrin had just popped out to do her grocery shopping. There were only hiking trails to and from the house. Dr. Perrin did not drive, preferring to teleport for any sort of movement she needed to do.

I cupped the pale yellow light in my hand closer to my chest, protecting the spell with my body. I moved forward slowly, scanning the ground for any irregularities, checking my hand every few seconds for a change of color of the spell in my hand. Nothing. I crept closer.

From the bend in the track, the house was nearly invisible until you were about 20 yards from the lower entrance. The house was built up against low hill, facing west. All three floors were filled with windows that looked out onto the lake. Due to the lush foliage, huge trees, and natural barrier of the hill, it was easy to miss the place until you were right on top of it. Which meant that if some danger were waiting for me, I would only have seconds to react.

Seeing nothing to make me take more caution and having no change in my spell, I moved forward a little more recklessly. It seemed to me that if there were no sign of human presence, then something had already happened to Dr. Perrin and there was nothing I could do at this point.

Unharmed, I made it to the clearing at the base of the house. Standing in the shelter of the trees I watched the house.

The sun was just coming over the back of the house, illuminating the lake in front. The windows of the house itself was still in shadow. There were no lights visible through the windows. I could see nothing wrong with the house—no broken windows, no forced doors, no holes in the roof. My spell held a steady yellow, but deep down I knew the infallibility of the spell. A clever witch could easily disguise herself from such a spell. I closed my hand to extinguish it.

I stepped away from the shelter of the trees and made my way, as quietly and quickly as I could muster, towards the house. I debated with myself while I crossed the clearing whether or not to knock on the door. But upon reaching the door, I walked right in without a second of hesitation.

The inside was as quiet as the outside. The air was stale and musty and from the feeble light coming in through the dirty windows the place looked as deserted as any dwelling could be. Dusty and unkempt, it looked as if no one had been in there for years. I stifled a snort of laughter. Dr. Perrin, brilliant researcher, horrible housekeeper. I made my way towards the stairs to living quarters on the second floor.

Had I not known the doctor at all, I would have assumed that an act of violence had taken place on the second floor. The kindest way to describe it would be 'sty.' How was any one supposed to know if something bad had happened to Dr. Perrin if you couldn't even tell the couch from the table?

Sighing with only a tiny bit of disgust, I quickly looked through the living area, the kitchen and the one bedroom and bathroom. Nothing but a huge mess. I made for the stairway to the upper floor, Dr. Perrin's laboratory.

The landing at the top of the stairs opened up into one large room. As my head became level with the floor of the top story I was beginning to wonder if Dr. Perrin hadn't gone on vacation and just hadn't told anyone. Her lab was in perfect shape. Immaculately clean and filled with cabinets and curios. Shiny instruments of infinite variety were neatly lined up along the counters and shelves.

Disappointed, I finished my climb to the top of the stairs. I knew I wasn't going to find Dr. Perrin, but I thought I would have a look around anyway. My disappointment dispersed almost immediately as I crossed the threshold into the lab. An icy wind hit me from all sides and I knew instinctively that I had set off a booby trap.

I danced the to the side and placed my back against a wall. In my haste I knocked off several frames from the wall. As they clattered around my ankles I took in the room around me. Nothing, yet. But that icy wind was portent of a powerful spell. I wished, unsuccessfully, for the sun to come around to the front of the house so I would have better light. The shadows might kill me for all I knew.

I strained my eyes searching for whatever would be coming. In only a few moments three forms began to take the shape of a human at each side of the room away from the doorway. As their solidity coalesced, so did the bright ball of power in what would be their hands.

"Shades," I said aloud even though the forms had no capac-ity for hearing. There was no wonder why I hadn't discerned any living person. Shades were a powerful spell, a shell of a person left behind as a form of protection. Or in this case, a form of assassin.

In the seconds I had until the Shades released their volley of spells that, at the very least, would maim or kill, I worked on generating my best shield spell. A master spell using a celtic rune, the protector, the sign of my grandmother's clan. It had never failed me. Yet now, I couldn't get it to take shape. There wasn't enough time.

Before I could work out my defenses, the first shade launched a fiery ball of energy at me. In desperation I called up an every day shield spell, one that I used on the subway to keep the mashers away. Spreading my hands before me, I generated a few square feet of energy. The fire bounced off and crashed into the floor, extinguishing itself.

Almost sighing with relief, I turned my attention to the other two Shades whose forms were now complete. I knew I couldn't use that simple spell for an all out assault. I could almost feel the fourth shade drawing itself up behind me to block the staircase. A quick look over my shoulder, around the doorframe, confirmed my suspicions.

Just then the Shade to my left let fly its spell. I ducked and rolled coming up in the middle of the room. The third Shade threw its spell at me. To avoid it I jumped as high as I could, flipping in mid-air. As I landed I let the momentum of the flip carry me forward. I knew I was just seconds away from being blown away by the fourth Shade and the next volley of spells from the first three were already regenerating. I let fly a spell of my own that shattered the windows ahead.

Running with full force I made for the opening. A fall of 50 feet was ahead of me, but none of the Shades could leave the room. It was my only chance of escape.

Just feet from the window I recalled a spell I had made up as a kid that allowed me to jump easily across rooftops. It was just the thing to carry me past the window for a fall in the lake. I sprang from the window practically screaming the spell.

I didn't fall. At least not straight down. I fell in a slow arc that curved over the yards from the house to the lake and brought me down as gently as a feather forty feet into Lake Geneva.

I was so relieved to have escaped unharmed from the Shades that I only took a second to grimace over the fact that I was swimming in Lake Geneva—a lake so polluted people weren't even allowed to boat in it. I looked towards the house and could easily pick out the broken window I had jumped through. From so far away I could not make out the Shades that must still be inside.

A Shade was the whisper of a person usually left as a guard or a fail-safe. They generally only had one spell and a limited number of times they could use it. If I guessed correctly, all four of those Shades had been from the same person and were packing some pretty powerful magic. There were only a handful of witches who could perform such a spell, or one group of malicious witches who could manage it together.

Swallowing a great gulp of air, I began my swim ashore. I made for the bank on the other side of the hill from Dr. Perrin's house. Once ashore, after gagging on the tiny amount of water I accidentally swallowed, I teleported directly back to headquarters.

"Notify Mistress immediately," I gasped aloud. "Dr. Perrin is missing and her laboratory is being guarded by shades." The night clerk's eyes widened in alarm and only hesitated a moment before she went into the closet behind her desk and sounded the on-alert alarm. I could hear the eerie sound of the crystal bowl vibrating its message. Half the staff and all senior staff would be arriving in a few minutes. I realized I was dripping wet still and made for the showers.

"Tell Mistress I'll be waiting in her office."

Chapter 6

Washington, D.C. and Hermance, Geneva, the Swiss/French Border

June 20, 1959

In less than a half hour, I found myself at the head of the staff table next to Mistress in the conference room with most of the senior staff and agents assembled. The French delegation had just arrived in the entrance hall.

I felt much better after getting cleaned up and changed. I had shared, via crystal exchange, with Mistress the event and that in itself was a large relief. It was similar to Witness, except that it was my real memories with all the distortions of fear and adrenaline mixed in. More experience than fact.

My AMIS colleagues were chatting quietly in their seats. Mistress wore a mask of steel, her posture ramrod straight, her hands firmly gripping her cane before her. I didn't even pretend to have that kind of strength. My mind was too boggled by the ramifications of the morning's events. At least it was Mistress who would face the French delegation, who were more than likely enraged and offended by AMIS's over-reaching investigation.

The open doors of the conference room were suddenly crowded by the three governing members of the Legation Francois Mysterious and several agents. The Legation was governed by a triumvirate of equals—that organization's founding tenants being a hold-over from the original French Revolution. However equal the three Directors were meant to be, everyone knew that there was one true leader. Madame Picard, of course, was at the head of the small party. She was the equal of Mistress in everything but talent. Her two "equal" directors, Madame Poulain and Madame Anrei, stood a pace behind her. I did not know the additional three agents in attendance.

Mistress waited at the head of the room for the delegation to reach her. Their seats had already been arranged at the head of the table. Madame Picard slowed as she reached the table. She and Mistress had a stare-down that had everyone in the room smoothing down their hair. I was once again glad for the intercession of Mistress. It's not that I was scared of Madame Picard–Mistress was far scarier–but she was not a compromising person and had always had a sincere dislike for me.

"Mistress," Madame Picard bowed her head slightly in greeting. Mistress bowed back, a little more deeply. Witches and magic users do not touch each other willingly. You never knew what charms or counter-spells might be waiting.

Mistress then began in, what was for her, a conciliatory tone, "I apologize for overstepping our agreed upon boundaries this morning." Madame Picard's cheeks began to pull into a slight, cruel smile. "However, under the circumstances you can see why I ordered the operation." The smile fell into a frown of consternation. "There is a most dire plot in action, Madame Picard, and I believe we would do well to work with one another to solve it."

There was nothing else Madame Picard could do but acquiesce. "Now," Mistress continued, "Esmeralda, please be so good as to describe for all present what happened this morning when you entered Dr. Perrin's fortified home.

I did my best to accurately describe the events of the morning. I was grateful for having shared with Mistress already. It seemed to have sharpened and cleared my memory, so that I was able to describe everything down to the smallest movement.

Elena, Mistress's junior secretary who was relegated to note taking for this meeting, gasped a little when I described my jump from the window, but everyone else was as silent as the grave. I felt as if someone had put a focus charm on the room. Mistress probably had.

When my narrative was over. The whole room visibly let their shoulders down. Madame Poulain and Madame Anrei shared a mutual look of apprehension behind Madame Picard's back.

"Let us now discuss what is to be done to investigate," started Mistress.

Before anyone could say anything else, Madam Picard began, "However important the rest of the investigation is, it was far outside the agreed on terms of jurisdiction, and we must, therefore, discuss reparations and . . ."

"My dear Suzanne," Mistress interrupted, "As our beloved Dr. Perrin's fate is in jeopardy, we should not take time to lay blame. I take full responsibility." Mistress's voice was poisonous and deadly. Madame Picard was not pleased but acquiesced to Mistress's demands. Mistress resumed directing the meeting.

Only a short while later, I found myself again facing the long track to Dr. Perrin's home. Legation had already commenced plans to send in their crack AST—anti-spell team—to deal with the Shades. They were also assembling a clean-up team, under the personal direction of Madame Poulain, to investigate Dr. Perrin's property.

I was assigned to be the point woman for the AST, so that they could follow exactly the route I took. After some finagling between Mistress and Madame Picard about who should be controlling overall operations for the joint venture, Mistress assigned most of the other senior agents to following-up with our world-wide informants.

Legation had closed down the small side road between Hermance and the border frontier a mile further down. Assembled at the head of the path to Dr. Perrin's house were a dozen Legation agents, a large van, and myself.

It took the AST team a half hour to crack a hole in the perimeter defenses. I could, of course, walk right in, but the half dozen members of the AST were not so privileged. I spent the half hour watching the team closely. For all intents and purposes it looked as if I were observing spell casting, but really I was trying to distinguish one team member from the other. Each woman was about 5 and a half feet tall, around 25 with light brown hair pulled tightly back into a bun. Each had eyes of an indistinguishable brown color. They were all slim and in excellent shape and while wearing their uniforms of gray jumpsuits, they all looked the same.

At one point, I wondered if the six women were some form of shade. But each spoke and acted independently—I was mostly sure. Finally I decided that they had been cast with some spell that made them all seem similar. Or maybe they just all did look the same.

A loud crack signaled that a doorway had been created. I felt a sickening quiver through my whole body at the breakage in the barrier. It was the effect of my own spell being cracked. I wondered if every other witch who helped create the barrier felt it too.

I walked right across the border of the barrier. Each AST member ducked through the lightly outlined crack. They assembled on the far side and I steeled myself to lead the way.

In another ten minutes we were nearing the house. Nothing was amiss, nothing had changed. My hand-held detection spell still showed that the house was empty of living humans. The six AST agents followed behind me loosely, now and then letting loose a spell of revelation or a charm of clarity on the forest surrounding the path. They were searching for additional boobytraps or jinxes. Their search was continually fruitless.

My skin prickled every time one of those searching spells was released and pinged away into the forest. My nerves were on edge and I couldn't help but grit my teeth. What a ludicrous situation I was in. Not seven hours later I found myself on the same walk. Why, I wondered, couldn't I still be living it up on the beach in Jamaica.

But I knew that there was no place I would rather be in the world than in the thick of the action as I was just then.

At the door of the house I came to a complete halt. Finally there was something wrong. It took me a few moments of remembering my original walk, but then I had it. When I had arrived at Dr. Perrin's door I had found it unlocked and closed. When I had entered the door I had left it open in case it became necessary to escape quickly.

To the AST agent immediately behind me I motioned to have her cast a detection spell on the doorway. "When I entered, I purposely left the door open. Someone has been here."

The agent nodded to me, silently. I watched her release a spark of light from her fingers and that flew towards the door with a hissing sound. The spark made a circuit of the door frame and a lazy circle around the knob before falling harm-lessly into the ground. The door was safe.

I decided that at this point the crack AST members should really earn their keep and take the lead. I took a rear position and followed them into the house. Nothing looked different to me and the two bottom floors were obviously safe. AST sent out spells and incantations in every direction with no results.

In the stairwell leading to the third floor landing, the half dozen AST members assembled into a formation that would allow them to enter the room and immobilize the shades. This was their key skill and they'd trained for it, in many cases, for years.

I hovered a few feet below the team straining to get a view of the third floor doorway. I could see nothing, no flicker or warble of a hovering shade. I even got a sense that nothing was up there, but I didn't want to be the one to test out that theory.

On a silent count of three, the AST leap into action and it was all over in an instant.

I bounded up the stairs to see the captured shades, but found, much to my dismay, that there was nothing to see. In fact there was nothing. Not only were the magicked guardians no longer acting watch guard over the lab, the lab had been cleared of all its equipment.

As I lingered, stunned, in the doorway, everyone of the AST members turned a frustrated gaze at me.

"Now what?" I asked no one in particular.

When I reported in person an hour and a half later, Mis-tress was not pleased.

"I knew I shouldn't have informed the Legation," Mis-tress spoke the word legation with such a sneer that the word became a slur. "I knew that horrid Madame Picard would ruin everything with her bureaucratic redundancy."

I then reported that the French investigative team had dis-covered the break in the spell-cast barrier that was supposed to have protected Dr. Perrin. The spelled barrier only went to the very lip of the shore, but not under the water. Whoever broke into the perimeters did it by digging out the soil on the bank allowing in a shallow inlet of water.

"Very clever indeed," was all that Mistress had to say in response. She leaned back in her chair, stroking the smooth wood on the armrests. I had not been invited to sit as of yet, but wanted nothing more than to lay on a couch and cover my eyes. It had been a crazy day, in many different time zones, and I was long past ready to sleep.

After five minutes of contemplation, Mistress spoke again. I had begun to nod off. I snapped my head up as Mistress's sharp voice broke the silence.

"Peter's clues are starting to come together, my dear. Agent Carmilla has been in touch with Rossini. It looks as though there is substantial Arcanimus activity in Damascus. Carmilla has set a meeting with Rossini in two days time. I want you to be the contact and find out as much as you can from them."

I nodded.

"I see that you are exhausted. Check in tomorrow afternoon by four o'clock for your briefing. The meeting is six a.m. our time, eleven local time. Get some rest now."

I didn't even have enough energy, or agility of thought, to think of a snappy goodbye. I just turned on my heel and left. And within 25 minutes of leaving Mistress's office, I was asleep in my own bed.

Chapter 7

Santorini, Aegean Sea

June 23, 1959

The salt air of the sea blew against my face as I sat underneath the canopy of a small café in Oia, a city on the Greek island of Santorini. The café had a spectacular view of the bay.

I looked out over the blue waters of the Southern Aegean Sea. Taking a deep breath of the warm salty air and I tried to relax into the laid back atmosphere of the island. Feeling the lure of waters that blue, I could understand why the ancient Greek seafarers had set out on their adventures.

I was more than an hour early for the meeting with Rossini. I sipped my sweet coffee slowly while reviewing the information I had received the afternoon before in my briefing with Mistress. The FBI had confirmed the handwriting on the note as that of Peter. Their deciphers had come to the conclusion that the words on the cigarette paper were:

> *Arcn.*
>
> *Iris prj.*
>
> *perrin*
>
> *damscus*
>
> *cosat*
>
> *jul II*

The translated writing didn't tell us too much we hadn't already found out. Arcanum, of course, who else would be plotting something? Iris Project. Mistress had heard only rumors. Perrin, Dr. Perrin, kidnaped or killed or something. Damascus, a clue that was corroborated by Carmilla's network of spies. And a date, July second, just a little over a week away.

I rubbed my temples trying to put order to the information we had already. Mistress, and many other field agents, had heard of a large undertaking by Arcanum. Under the direction of the ancient society's latest mistress, they were plotting to use some sort of spelled modern technology to amplify spell power. To me it sounded ridiculous, for I couldn't imagine what the use would be. But knowing Himiko as well as I did, I knew the plan must be meticulously thought out and dire in consequences.

Himiko was a tremendously powerful witch, perhaps as strong as even Mistress. Someone as strong as Himiko would have no problem creating a few shades to guard Dr. Perrin's top floor laboratory.

"Things are getting interesting," I said aloud as the pieces of the puzzle began forming a picture.

Himiko's story was a unique and a bittersweet one. Himiko, just like me, came into her magic early and strong. Her mother, Sachiko, was chief witch to the Japanese Emporer, Hirohito. As Japan prepared its war machine in the 1930s it depended significantly on the aid of Sachiko to provide spells of stealth and force. Much like Hitler's Schutzstaffel Frauen aided the Blitzkrieg. Just after the invasion of China, it was discovered that Sachiko had relied on Himiko's power to make those most potent of spells. This discovery led to Himiko's being the primary force behind Japan's invasion of South East Asia. Her spells of stealth were unmatched. Sachiko's powers had been dwindling with her own poor health and when she died in 1938 she left Himiko in the hands of Japan's warmongers, a 8 year-old-girl.

Himiko was isolated in a castle in Nara and forced to do the bidding of the army chiefs. She was never mistreated, but she was not allowed to talk to anyone but her masters and could never question their authority.

The witch community around the world knew of the powerful Sachiko and her daughter. And it didn't take much to realize, after Sachiko's death, who now magicked Japan to numerous battle victories.

I knew Himiko, knew what she went through. In 1943, at the height of World War Two, Vadim and I liberated Himiko ourselves. It was like two teenagers helping their friend escape for a night on the town. Except that the fate of the world was the result of that particular break-out.

Vadim and I, my closest friend from childhood, devised a plot to get to Himiko. I had guessed that Himiko didn't naturally partake in the war effort, but was being forced. Afterall, what child would want to do something so boring as sit alone in a castle and aide the war effort? We had planned to break in to the castle keep and find out if she really wanted to be there. Turned out, she was glad to go. Himiko stayed with me under the supervision of Mistress at first, so I got to know her, as much as anyone could.

In early 1946, after Japan was thoroughly, irrevocably defeated, Himiko disappeared. She was only 16. I wondered if she went back to Japan. A witch as powerful as she is would be safe wherever she went, but Vadim and I often wondered if she could be happy. Neither of us understood why she left. Soon after that I joined up with the service as a full-fledged member and Vadim went his own way. It wasn't until six years later that we found that Himiko had joined the Arcanimus and was steadily rising through its ranks.

Sitting in that pleasant café, I had closed my eyes as I remembered how I had broken in to the castle in Nara. Smiling slightly, I couldn't believe how brazen I had been at just fourteen. Luck really had been on my side that day. As well as for Vadim.

Vadim! I wasn't supposed to be able to remember him. I frowned as I scanned my surroundings. I wore a charmed ring to keep me from thinking of him. I fingered the nearly invisible, usually forgotten, ring on the middle finger of my right hand. If it was working properly, the only time I would even know I had it on, remember what I tried so hard to forget, was when Vadim was nearby.

"Drats!" I muttered. The waitress was walking by and looked at me with a questioning face. "It just figures that he'd show up when there is some action."

Surreptitiously I looked around. The streets were very quiet. A few tourists browsing the shops and an elderly couple shared the shade of the canopy a few feet from me. I half-stood to peer down the steep streets below, but caught no sight of him. I sat back in the chair and fanned myself, the heat unexpectedly starting to weigh on me. I let my eyes rest on the blue of the sea and tried to go back to my reasoning of the problem at hand. If Vadim were nearby, it was none of my concern. At least, I told myself that it was none of my concern.

I picked up where I had left off. Himiko. What could Himiko be plotting? Since she had made a coup for leadership some four years before, she had been relentless in building up Arcanimus's ranks and resources. For example, the selling of arcane weapons to the Chinese. And there had been dozens of such incidents recently.

I could understand kidnaping Dr. Perrin. After all, the woman was a genius. "If I were running an evil secret society," I thought, "I would do anything to get Dr. Perrin to work for me."

That lead me back to whatever the Iris Project is. Whatever Himiko is planning, if it is the Iris Project, then she must have needed Dr. Perrin's unmatched magical research abilities to complete it. That gave me a little hope. It would take something beyond the force of nature to make Dr. Perrin do something she did not wish too. It also meant that Himiko was failing to make the project work herself. I smiled as I thought of the temper tantrum Himiko would throw if she couldn't magic it herself. She wasn't used to failing.

Suddenly I felt a jolt of the feelings that I had been repressing for years. Vadim was very near now. I sighed knowing that inevitably I would have to see him. I pulled out my compact and lipstick. While checking my make-up I contacted Mistress.

"Yes, dear?" came Mistress's tiny voice. "Have you already met with Rossini?"

"No, not yet. I'm waiting at the rendezvous point. I was wondering if anyone knew what Dr. Perrin had been researching or developing in the last few months. Is there anyone who might?"

Mistress looked away for a few seconds and then back at the mirror. "I've asked that question of Madame Picard myself. No one seems to know. However," Mistress continued with a twitch of her lips that could be a smile, "I know one person who wouldn't be questioned by the Legation, but whom I might be able to charm with my wits and stunning personality."

"Just don't do anything I wouldn't." I smiled at the joke. I couldn't help but respect the old woman's spunk. "Also, I thought you should know, Vadim is nearby. Probably here for the same reason as me."

Mistress frowned. "Take care of yourself, Esmeralda. Please think before you ..."

Mistress's admonition was cut short by the timely shutting of the compact. Vadim had just come around the corner of the café and made straight for my table, stopping a few feet away. Probably as a caution, given my sometimes uneven temper. Very wise, really. He was not surprised to see me, not at all. I guessed he'd been listening nearby.

"Hello, Esme, you look wonderful" he spoke in his native Russian. He looked down at the compact in my hand. "And how is Mistress?"

I tightened my lips in an effort to control my words. I answered in English, "Mistress is unchanging, you know that. Thank you for the compliment. You look well too."

Tall and lean, blonde and handsome, Vadim gracefully crossed the few feet that separated us, pulled out a chair and sat down face-to-face from me. My heart was doing flip-flops in my chest and I struggled to control my breathing. An unfortunate effect of the memory charm. Once it is weakened, the bearer felt a flood of the memories and emotions that had been suppressed.

We stared at each other in silence for a moment. I was too conflicted to speak just yet, and when I did speak I wanted to be able to say something pithy and smart. Vadim just looked at me, his eyes lit up.

My hand lay on the table. Vadim reached across and put his fingers over my memory charm. "You shouldn't wear one of these if you can't take the after effects."

I yanked my hand from under his and put it in my lap. I slipped the ring off and stuck it in my pocket. When I was finally able to breathe regularly again, all I felt was a deep and sincere desire to win.

"I don't suppose you're here as a tourist?" I asked hopefully.

Vadim shook his head slightly, "No. You?" He raised his eyebrows expectantly.

I also shook my head. "Rossini?"

"Yes."

We fell silent again. I wanted so much to be able to speak with him openly, to ask him how his life was, to find out if he was married, if he was happy. I wished I could connect with him as the friend I had known nearly my whole life. But I couldn't. Too much had changed, too much time had passed. What remained was the competitiveness we always had as children.

"How are things in Moscow?" I asked casually.

Vadim shrugged his shoulders. "Fine, I should think. I don't spend much time there. Still have the same apartment in New York?"

"No, I've moved to a bigger place. Plus my former neighbors started to get suspicious about my comings and goings. And the loud thumps every time I leaped in."

Vadim laughed a little at my description. I continued, "How are things at KGBB? Still with the agency I presume."

"You would be the first to know if I were not." KGBB—Committee for State Magic Security—was the USSR's counterpart to AMIS. KGBB was one of the only government magic agencies that was dominated by male members. During the 18th and 19th centuries, the Czars had run a program to "breed" magic into males. The program was roundly denounced as unethical, but what was done was done. Vadim was a direct descendent of one of the successes and was a very powerful sorcerer.

"What's it been, six years since we saw each other last?" Vadim began.

"Don't. Let's not talk about anything personal," I said. "Let's not talk about anything."

Vadim only nodded and continued to look at me. I turned my head to look at the blue sea.

I thought about the games Vadim and I had played as children, so innocent and happy. Well, innocent of the political struggles we would later know. Neither of us had ever played fair. I let myself, just for a second, miss my childhood, remember my mother.

Vadim looked away from me. "I was most unhappy to hear about your mother's disappearance." I nodded, whether he noticed or not I did not know. "I like to think that both our mother's are living it up in their later years on a beach resort in Tahiti."

I couldn't help but smile at the picture. "My mother would be flirting with every young man she met, breaking a new heart everyday."

"And my mother would be comforting the broken-hearted in her own fashion." Both of us laughed ruefully. Vadim's mother, Tola, and Birgitta had been close friends. Tola, a Polish-national witch, was one of the seamstresses that toured with the opera company. Vadim's father, a Russian ballet master, was also part of the group. My mother and Tola had been friends for years, but became very close when they both had their only child within a year of each other. Vadim's father fell victim to an assassination in the early 1930s. Tola had disappeared during the last days of the War.

Both of us fell silent again. There was too much sad history between us. After a few minutes an elderly woman hobbled towards the café. She stopped only when she reached our table.

"Hello Daria," I said quietly. I smiled at the old woman. Vadim nodded at her.

"Good morning to you," Daria said in heavily accented English. "You are the young couple wanting for the tour?"

"Ah, yes, of course," I improvised. "Are you our guide?"

"No, no," laughed Daria. "I shall take you to the meeting point."

I left some money on the table and Vadim and I both stood and followed Daria. For an old woman, she ambled very quickly. We were soon past the out buildings of the town and going beside a dusty road between lush vineyards. Daria led the way, Vadim and myself walking behind her. Now and then Daria would say something over her shoulder, but as it was rhetorical, neither of us felt compelled to answer.

About a mile out of the town, we turned down a lane that led first to the vineyard warehouses and then up a steep incline to a grand house. Daria led us into the second warehouse building and down a dark, old staircase to the cold storage rooms below.

"You'll be meeting with Taddeo. He manages the route into Syria." Daria said as she led us down the ill-lit stairway. I could smell better than I could see. I smelled cool earth, old wet wood, and sweet wine that had gone to vinegar.

As we neared the room below, it became lighter. Once down on the floor, the cellar was about 50 feet long and 20 feet wide. A part of it was taken up by large, oak wine casks. The rest of the space was filled with boxes and crates.

At the far end was a short ramp that led up to the open doors of the cellar. Men went in and out carrying large heavy boxes from the cellar to the open bay of a small truck. The real purpose of Rossini was smuggling.

Rossini was not a person. Rossini was the known name of the largest smuggling and black market operators in the Mediterranean. Operating from their home base on Santorini and several other islands strung out from the Aegean to Gibraltor, Rossini dominated the unlicensed shipping trade. More than a century old, the group was named for its aide to the Italian anarchist movement in the 19th Century. Italian officials called them Red for aiding the revolutionaries. It was all the same to the smugglers however. They would have dealt with government officials, or even the pope himself, if any of them had had a need for their services.

Rossini were so dominant in their business because the organization, in fact the family, was largely endowed with magic. Strong witches ran in the family and their specialty always seemed to be subterfuge and confusion. No one could cast a charm of cloudy mind like a Rossini. Their unofficial family name was widely known to people who had no concern in their affairs. But any official or competitor who wanted to remember would immediately forget—even forget that the organization existed. It was a mighty spell that the whole family of witches cast. So powerful that any mundane municipality or government who wanted to stop these masterful operators would hardly get down the first letter R on their notepad before they remembered that they had left the stove on and had to hurry home.

Rossini was widely known among the magical community, government-oriented or civilian alike. The magical community were blind to Rossini's illegal operations, not just out of loyalty to a fellow magic workers, but because of their trading practices. They were amazing sources of information. The organization never took sides, and treated each government equally. The Third Reich even left them alone, although they were the primary supplier of black market goods to Europe during the war years.

Once Daria, Vadim and I were all inside the cellar, Daria turned to the right and led us to a small office shielded by the stairway. Two men were leaning over a table with a large map spread between them. They were speaking a dialect of Greek that I didn't know. Upon noticing that there were visitors, the two men looked up. The older of the two folded the map and walked out of the little office, nodding hello to the visitors.

"Take care of the children, Taddeo," Daria said with a wave of her hand as she turned to go.

Taddeo waved us inside and bade us sit at the table. He is a lean, middle-aged man with thinning hair, but a personality as forceful as steel battering ram. "I'm glad you've come," Taddeo now spoke in Italian—a language in which both Vadim and I were fluent. "Time is getting close I think."

"I'm sure you both have heard something of Arcanimus's latest plans?" Vadim and I eyed one another suspiciously, professional competition holding steady.

"I see you have," Taddeo continued. "One of our traders comes through Damascus where a fortune-telling witch allows us to use the back of her shop for storage."

"A real witch or fake?" I inquired.

"Real, not particularly talented, mind you, but very efficient in the fogging of the mind spells. They work well even on other witches."

"That's quite a talent. She hasn't been recruited for any national operations?" I interrupted again.

Taddeo gave my a sharp look to silence me. "She likes her independence, let's say. She lives in the old city near the Roman gate. About ten months ago a hive of Arcanimus set up shop in an abandoned house a few doors away from her. When they came around to check up on her abilities she played mundane. So far they haven't been suspicious."

"She's been monitoring their movements. At first she thought they might be moving in on Rossini territory, but it looks like they have different plans. She believes there are eleven members living there, including one that matches the description of Himiko. Three nights ago, there was a late-night delivery of two huge crates. Our spy took a look down the cellar and found a large lab installed in one of the sub-floors. She doesn't know what were in the crates or if anything was brought in, but she knows that they are getting ready to move within the next week."

Vadim and I shared a look. "Dr. Perrin?" I asked. Vadim nodded.

"Whatever is going on, you two need to put an end to it. Having the Arcanimus so close to our operations is not safe."

"We can go right now," I stood up. Taddeo held his hand flat out indicating I should sit down.

"You can't just jump there. Our spy believes the Arcanimus have alarms all over the city. They are well guarded against any magic use near to them. Our witch has disabled more than two herself. If you enter the city magically, you'll be giving yourself away."

"Fine I'll just . . ."

"Will you be patient for one second?" Taddeo snapped at me. "We've got this worked out for you already. We did the hard work. You just get to go for a ride."

I slumped in my chair feeling like a school-child who'd been scolded by the teacher.

"Now, I'm taking a shipment to the port at Jubayl. There you can ride in the truck of our man into Damascus. We leave at high tide and you'll be in the city before midnight tomorrow. Got it."

"That's too long!" I protested. "If they have Dr. Perrin, we need to get there yesterday."

This time it was Vadim who stopped me. "Even you aren't that good," he gave me a crooked smile. "He's right Esme. Just let it be. If we jump in, we'll be putting the good Doctor into more trouble than she is already."

I fumed, probably at least as much for his condescending remarks as for calling me by me childhood name.

"Fine, I'll go along quietly, but I hate waiting."

Taddeo looked relieved. Rossini had as much riding on this as I did. They wouldn't want their "storage space" or their spy compromised by my thoughtless actions. "You can rest up in the bunks upstairs. We'll have dinner before we go. I'll call you then."

Daria appeared in the doorway and motioned us to follow her. She led us both back up the narrow staircase and from the storehouse where we entered, she took us up another two flights of stairs to a long low room. It was the attic space directly under the roof eaves and it was very hot. But windows at both ends of the room caught some of the island trade winds cooling it to a tolerable degree. It was lined with chairs, tables and cots.

Once Daria had us both in the room she turned and went back down the stairs. Vadim immediately threw himself down on a cot, tucking his arms behind his upturned head. I felt uncomfortable. It was ridiculous that I should have to spend a boring afternoon in this infernal attic. It was also extremely rude to make me partner up with Vadim.

"For heaven's sake, he's my sworn enemy!" I thought as I turned my back on him and went to the West facing window. I took out my compact thinking of how I could contact Mistress without Vadim overhearing. I decided I'd take a walk and headed for the stairs.

"If we were supposed to walk around they wouldn't have put us up here." Vadim said without even turning his head.

I pursed my lips in frustration. I was sorely tempted to leap right out of there back to Mistress's office. The only thing that kept me from doing it was the fear that the place was enchanted to disallow teleportation. If that were the case, I would only humiliate herself in front of Vadim.

While I hesitated at the top of the stairs, Vadim spoke again, "If you really need to run to Mistress and tell her everything, you can put an ear wax charm on me while you speak."

I grew very close to throwing a tantrum. Stalking noisily to the other side of the room, as far from Vadim as I could get, and fell into a chair banging my back needlessly. We each stayed in our respective spots for the long afternoon. Vadim slept effortlessly. I dozed off but always hit my chin on my chest. After awhile I just gave up and just watched the sunlight play on the ocean.

Late in the afternoon I heard Vadim stir and then get up. Without turning around I said, "Perhaps we should consult."

During the long afternoon, I realized that I had been really frustrated with the investigation. With Vadim showing up out-of-the-blue and the rush of feelings as my remembering charm broke, I had let myself be reduced to childish behavior. I could do better than that. It was obvious that Vadim was looking into the Arcanimus himself, otherwise he wouldn't be here. I needed to buck up and do my job—despite the animosity I was feeling towards him.

He pulled up a chair next to mine. "What would you like to know?"

I refrained from rolling my eyes at him. He always could get to me, even more so than Mistress. "You know about Dr. Perrin, you know about Peter. What led you to Rossini?"

Vadim turned towards me, trying to read my profile. "Yes, we had heard about both incidents." He was quiet for a moment, but I didn't look to see why. "I was sorry to hear about Peter. But I'm glad you took Witness even though it must have been hard for you." Again he was silent. "Peter didn't deserve to die that way."

The sun was low on the horizon, it would soon be time to head out across the Eastern Mediterranean to Syria. I was doing my best to remain calm.

"I came to the Rossini because we know that Arcanimus are working on a high-level security project that is to come to fruition by next month."

"Would that be the Iris Project?" I interjected.

Vadim raised his eyebrows. "Yes, that is the name we too have heard. But how...?"

"It was written on the note that Peter handed me before trying to escape his pursuers."

"Ah yes, we heard there were some clues. Do you know what it is? Was there any description?"

"None. What do you know of it?"

"We got wind of the Iris Project about three weeks ago. Arcanimus members infiltrated our space exploratory program and the launch pad at the Cosmodrome. They did not know that there was an agent of KGBB present who watched for glamour spells. He saw right through the glamours of the women visiting the outpost. He overheard them mention this project but only as they were leaving. The only specific information he heard was the mention of a satellite being prepared in time."

I turned that information over in my mind for a moment. "If they are building a satellite, then they must be thinking of hijacking a rocket launch. . ." I grew excited as I began to put the information together. "The only two places in the world they can launch rockets into orbit would be Baikonur or in Cape Canaveral!"

The excitement of finally having something concrete to work with brought me out of my chair. Vadim laid his hand on my arm to calm me down. "We don't know which one, we don't know when, and we don't know why."

I looked at him with a triumphant smile, "But we do know when." I then explained to him all of the details in Peter's note.

"It still doesn't explain why."

I sighed with dismay. "But we know when and what. Where shouldn't be too hard since our choices are so narrow. Why doesn't really matter as long as we stop them."

I folded my arms in a petty gesture. Vadim laughed his quiet laugh. "We'll have more answers after we get to Damascus."

Thinking of the expedition to Damascus brought out the professional in me. And the planning of our mission took over my mind.

Chapter 8

Damascus, Syria

June 24, 1959

After a large, greek-style dinner, that left me so full I felt like I could sleep for days, I found myself in the berth of a small fishing boat. As Taddeo had packed the small vessel full of contraband, there was very little room for comfort, or even movement, below deck. Taddeo had been kind enough to leave a small gap open between stacks of crates which created a short bench on which Vadim and I both sat.

I was bent over my glamour, working it's spell—a little groggy from the wine I had drunk with dinner. Vadim was doing the same. We had decided that we would both disguise ourselves as Arab merchants and we would use full-body glamour suits rather than just the disguising spell. If the defenses around Damascus were as tight as Taddeo claimed, then the glamour suits would be least detectable. We had thought about going as ourselves—pretending to be a married couple on holiday. However, we would not have the freedom of movement in the old city that we would have as Arab men.

Once we had lodged ourselves in the boat that evening, we each had worked on constructing our own spell. Taddeo had offered the required clothing. All that was left to cast would be the language spell, so that we spoke the proper dialect of Arabic, and that would have to wait until we were close to docking in Syria.

I finished my glamour and shook it out by the shoulders, only slightly trying to impress Vadim with my quick handiwork. Then I folded it neatly and laid it across my lap. Stretching and yawning, the long day had caught up with me. We weren't due to dock until afternoon, some twelve hours later. Nothing left to do but sleep, I leaned against the nearest crate and settled in.

Within a few minutes Vadim had finished his glamour as well. He stood and said he was going above deck. I gave a slight nod and fell deeply asleep.

When I woke, what must have been many hours later, my face was pressed against Vadim's chest as he cradled me in his arms. Half asleep still, I nestled into his comfortable arms. But it was only a second longer before I realized where I was and struggled to sit bolt upright. Unfortunately, I had been curled up on the small bench and the sudden, unplanned movement sent me backward off the seat. Vadim woke with a start nearly tumbling off the seat himself.

Collecting himself he looked down and laughed as I rubbed the back of my head. Not only had landed hard on my backside, I had also thumped my head against the neighboring crate.

"How did you do that?" Vadim asked innocently enough. I just scowled at him. He gave me a hand up and sat me next to him on the bench. Embarrassed, I stood up and looked up through the hatch to hide my feelings.

"The sun is coming up. It must be about six."

"Only six hours to go then." Vadim replied with a yawn.

"What are we supposed to do? I don't get why we can't just jump to the sea port when we need to." The statement was rhetorical. My frustrations always grew when I was embarrassed.

"I guess we'll just have to enjoy each other's company." I glared at him, even more frustrated that he could be so natural around me, as if nothing had happened at all.

Vadim reached into his inner pocket and pulled out a playing card. Once it was cupped in his hand, the single card became a full pack of cards. "Gin Rummy?"

I readily agreed and helped pull a crate closer to us to use as a table. Taddeo brought some breakfast a short while later and we made ourselves as comfortable, and occupied, as we could for the rest of the trip.

It was nearly noon when the small fishing boat reached the edges of the port near to Jubayl on the Lebanese coast. Vadim had watched through a porthole as we passed the break water. "Time to get ready."

We slipped on our guazy, shimmery glamour suits. I found the tall, yet portly, man suit much more comfortable than the tiny Chinese man I had worn a few weeks before. I had purposely made my suit a little large so I could wear my own clothing underneath. There was no way I was going to get caught out naked if I had to ditch the suit fast. Vadim stripped down to his undershorts before slipping the suit on. I tried not to notice.

Once the suits were adjusted and the proper clothing on, we spelled each other with the language spells. It was much easier to perform on someone else's vocal chords than on your-self. In no time at all, Vadim was cracking jokes in rural Arabic about goats and I was laughing in a high-pitched school boy giggle, not the least becoming to my glamour.

It was more than an hour later when we were escorted off the boat. Many of the boxes had already been removed before Taddeo came below deck to escort us to our next conveyance.

He laughed when he saw us, his eyes sparkling. "You both have missed your calling doing spy work. You should work for me. I could use your disguise making skills." Chuckling as he turned, we followed him off the boat.

I was not pleased at the look of the truck we were to ride in, but I remained silent as I followed Taddeo. He led us to up to the back of an old pre-war-style truck that had no paint left on it. Even before it was fully loaded it leaned uneasily to the left. On the bed of the truck, tucked just below the back window was a small built-in cabin. Taddeo indicated to us that this is where we were to ride.

"After you my dear," Vadim said gallantly.

"Thank you I'm sure," I replied as I hauled my chubby fake body up into the bed of the truck. I squeezed in through the opening and didn't find the accommodations any more pleas-ing. But there was nothing for it. Sitting, I found that I could just sit up straight, my head just touching the top of the cabin. My legs were short enough that I could stretch them out. Poor Vadim, I thought, is going to be mighty uncomfortable.

A second later, Vadim had crawled inside. We sat with our backs against the cabin of the truck. Vadim, even in his suit which was several inches shorter than his actual height, didn't have enough clearance to sit-up. He rounded his back and folded up his legs as best he could.

Taddeo stuck his head in and smiled a bit ungraciously at his passengers. "Well, you fit in there alright. This truck is going directly to the fortune-teller's cellar. Naji here," he pointed to the man invisible behind him, "will be your courier. We're now going to pack in the crates around you, so you'll be sealed in. You should be off within the hour and the ride to Damascus will take about ..." he turned and whispered to the man behind him, "about six or seven hours. Good luck." Taddeo finished with a smirk.

The man who must be Naji stuck his head in. "Hello there! Glad to have you aboard. Sorry for the cramped space, but what can you do?" he raised his shoulders to his ears. He handed in a large clasped bottle. "Water for the trip. I'll make it as fast as I can." Saying no more, Naji cleared the doorway and placed a large board in front of it. It was very stuffy and hot with only a dim bit of light from the slats in the wooded sideboards.

Vadim and I were silent as we heard and felt the truck being loaded with goods. After a while the sounds of people outside the truck diminished and then we heard the roar of the truck coming to life. An even more uncomfortable vibration ran along the truck bed as it took off down the road. I was seriously contemplating conjuring a seat cushion. A muffled groan came from Vadim on my left. I couldn't see him, but considering I fit in the small cabin and I was uncomfortable, I knew Vadim must be feeling the strain of it.

"At least its not excessively noisy as well." Vadim turned his head towards me and rested his cheek on his knees. I could just make out his profile. "Remember that time we tried to commandeer that munitions delivery truck in Belgium?"I asked.

"And we got locked in the iron trunk and couldn't get out." There was a hint of mirth in Vadim's reply.

During the war, we had often tried to help out the war effort for the Allies, and mostly just got into trouble. That time in Belgium, we thought we could disappear a large munitions delivery to Antwerst and wound up being trapped for the length of the ride. We found out the hard way just how bad the effects of iron on witchcraft could be. Neither of us could so much as get a spark of fire going.

"At least we're not captives this time." We both chuckled at the memory. "A few weeks back I was doing deep undercover–

the most boring assignment Mistress has ever given me. For two weeks I was living in a glamour suit the size of a small Chinese man. I was never so uncomfortable."

"Are you telling me this to make be feel more at ease?"

Why did Vadim always have to say what should have been implied, I thought. It made things so less civil. "I'm telling you to imply that I know how uncomfortable you must be right now."

Vadim reached out and squeezed my ankle. His comrade-like touch somehow made me feel less anxious.

"Why don't you try lying on your side with you knees tucked up?" I suggested. Vadim squirmed around until he was laying as I suggested.

"Much better."

"For you." I now sat with Vadim's nose at my hip and his knees tucked under my legs. "This won't do." I twisted and turned, leaned and prodded, until I was nose-to-knees with Vadim and he to me. "I don't know how long I'll be able to stay this way."

"Don't worry, we won't be in here long."

"Ha," I laughed at his optimism. He laughed too. We continued our trip down memory lane speaking to one another's shinbones, sharing memories and nearly forgotten memories, until the drone of the truck finally sent us to sleep.

I woke, who knows how long later, at the sudden quiet. It was now completely dark in the tiny cabin. The truck was stopped and men were speaking. I tensed. Vadim was awake too and responded the same. I knew this because his arm was hooked over my leg and when he tensed he suggestively squeezed my legs. I moved my leg to shoo him off, but he only squeezed harder. Pursing my lips to keep from swearing at him, I tried to remain calm. A moment later the truck started up again and we were once again moving.

"City checkpoint," Vadim stated. Now I kicked at him in earnest. He protested with an 'ouch' and leaned up on his elbow. "No need for such violence Miss O'Rourke."

"Give it up, we're almost there." And a few minutes later the truck slowed and then went into reverse on an incline. We could hear the truck being unloaded and finally the wood panel was removed and we were blinded by the low light of a storage room. Slowly we crawled out of our hiding space, each stretching and flexing our muscles and joints. Vadim rubbed vigorously the shoulder he had been laying on.

Naji waited patiently while we got used to standing up again. "Please, follow me." He turned and led us through a dank stone passage and up a short flight of stairs. At the top was waiting a very skinny old woman who was bedecked in flowing robes and golden jewelry. She wore a headscarf of a filmy material that was embroidered with tiny stars.

The old woman narrowed her shriveled eyelids and gave us a thorough appraisal. If she could see through our glamour suits, she didn't say. Somehow I knew that she could. "You can call me Mari." She walked away.

Vadim and I followed, each nodding at Naji as we passed. We wouldn't be seeing the smuggler again. We found her in the next room sitting behind a small table bearing a crystal ball.

"This is my safe room. We can speak of anything here without fear of any unwanted listeners." She swept her hand to the side indicating the chairs that we could use. I sat down and stretched my legs out in front of me. Vadim preferred to remain standing, flexing his arms now and then.

"Wouldn't a listener know that this room was spelled if it was silent while they tried to listen?" I asked.

"Any person trying to listen through a magical device or through a door would hear the muffled hoo haw that an," she inclined her head to show her distaste, "ungifted medium would be saying to her clients."

I raised my eyebrows, "That's quite a spell, Madame Mari. Quite an impressive spell in fact."

"It is old knowledge among my family. In the mountains of lower Kurdistan, there is not a dwelling that does not carry the spell—witched or regular." Mari had a gleam in her eye bearing her pride in her ancestry. "Enough of this. We need to get on with the affair at hand."

"I am glad that you come tonight, for it looks like they are on the move." Vadim and I exchanged worried glances. "A large truck has been blocking the alleyway behind their safe house since an hour before dark. It looks as if they may be moving."

"Where is it, show me." I said forcefully now standing at attention.

"Now now, you must see the interior," Mari replied, ignoring my rude demand. "Please sit and I will show you."

I pulled my chair close to the table, Vadim did likewise. Mari grasped the sides of the crystal ball and an instant later a memory appeared. Following the scene with intense concentration, I watched as the view changed from the outside of a building and wound its way past guarded doorways and locked doors. At the end, I knew how to get through the Arcanimus hive and that Dr. Perrin was held captive in the basement.

I was resolved to get in there immediately. Mari looked from my face to Vadim's. She stood and led the way through the house and out a doorway into a narrow street. "At that corner there, turn right. You shall see the truck, it has not left yet." Without another word, she stepped back into the house and softly closed the door.

"Pass by it?" Vadim mouthed. I nodded and we stepped out at an even saunter.

"Tell me Hakim," I ventured, "what did you think of the meeting with that furrier today? Think he'll give us a good price on the skins?"

Vadim answered by thoughtfully stroking his beard, we just crossed the threshold of the alley way. "Tell you what I think," we both looked down toward the large truck. The only visible person was someone leaning against a wall smoking. Man, woman, or witch, we could not tell, but the person never looked towards us. "I think that man is shady from toes to top, that's what I think." We continued down to the next street talking idly of our fictitious meeting with the furrier.

"One guard or are there more we can't see?" I asked breathlessly as we rounded the next block.

"One guard. The rest of the operatives are most likely working on what ever they are moving–whether its in or out."

I thought for a moment then a large smile spread over my bearded face. "How about a Confuse Mistress operation with a mist glamour on the guard?"

Vadim readily agreed. He leaned against the nearest building, took a quick look around to make sure no one else was on the street, then began the incantation in a low whisper. As he spoke, he started to fade. After no more than 10 seconds all you could see of him were the bricks behind him.

"Ready," came his disembodied voice. I turned back down the street, returning to my earlier conversation with Hakim. Vadim answered until about halfway down the street then said a hearty farewell just as the came to the alley corner. I turned and called out, "Hakim take care of those pretty daughters of yours. We'll talk about this more in the morning." With a wave, I turned and went towards the large truck, conjuring a cigarette from the pocket of the guard.

As I neared the listless guard who still hadn't bothered to look up, I hailed him, "Young man, ho ho! Can you offer a poor man a light for his cigarette?" I halted in front of the young man, who turned out to be a young woman with an ill-cast glamour. Sulkily she took out her matches and struck one for the dumpy middle-aged man in front of her. I formed the spell in my mind as I inhaled on the cigarette. As I exhaled, less than a foot from the guard, I allowed the spell to follow. The guard gave a little cough at the rude smoke in her face, but before she could protest I spoke in a low voice. "I was never here. You saw no man or woman come by for at least an hour. You are feeling very sleepy. Don't fall asleep, you will get into trouble."

Dropping the cigarette at my feet, I faced the entrance to the Arcanimus lair. No movement was detectable, so I entered. Whether Vadim entered before me or was coming in after me, I was not sure. Taking the doorway to the left, I found the staircase that Mari had shown us in the crystal ball.

At the bottom I found a sentry fast asleep standing up against the wall. I guessed that Vadim was ahead of me. I moved with more alacrity knowing that Vadim was clearing a path. As I neared the bottom level, I heard voices coming from above.

"Everything is ready, ma'am. The truck is loaded and secured."

"Good, the spell alarm has been tripped very near and I would prefer my plans remain a secret." My face contorted with silent rage. It was Himiko. She was there, just mere feet above me. Taking a breath, I continued to listen. "You've taken care of the building?"

"Once we leave any witch who enters the building will trip the explosives and the building will come down. I've already taken care of destroying the lab just in case the explosive charge does not reach the sub-basement."

"Well done, . . ." the sound of Himiko's voice was lost as she exited the stairwell. I was torn. Go after Himiko and use the one chance I had to try and apprehend her, or continue looking for Dr. Perrin? I tore off my glamour suit—the better to fight. I was just tensing my muscles for a dash up the stairwell, when I heard scuttling noises from the end of the corridor.

I had to help Dr. Perrin, I owed her that much.

I sprinted to the doorway at the end of the 10 foot corridor and threw it open. If Vadim were there I could not see him. The place was a mess. There was nothing left unbroken, untwisted, unturned. Only one dangling lightbulb cast a swaying shadow over the place. I scanned the room and saw no sign of life. Then it hit me—a cloud of poisonous air. I was only a few feet into the room and I had to back out quickly. I assessed the situation quickly enough. Vadim, invisible, was probably suffocating somewhere in the room.

Without another thought I said, "gas masks," and held out my open palms. Two state-of-the-art masks appeared. One in each hand. I put one over my head and scuffled into the room. My only hope of finding Vadim quickly was to slide my feet over the floor until I found him. He couldn't have gotten too far into the room before he passed out. With the clearer vision provided by the mask, I saw that the gas hovered at about waist level and higher. It gave me hope that Vadim would make it.

About fifteen feet into the room, I came across the first overturned table. It had been badly demolished with some sort of blasting spell—one corner had been twisted off. As I neared it, I saw on the other side Dr. Perrin looking for all the world to be dead.

Just then I shuffled into the invisible Vadim and fell over him. Quickly recovering, I turned and ran my hands over the length of him, or what I thought was the length of him, unraveling his spell, until he again became visible. He was still just a see through shadow, but that was all I needed. Clumsily I attached the other mask to his face. I turned him to face up and he took a few choking breaths but did not wake up.

I pulled his limp body as close to Dr. Perrin as I could, grabbing Dr. Perrin's hand. With an effort to concentrate I leapt, taking the two others to Mari's consultation room. The room was too small for the two prone forms and Vadim came down hard on the crystal ball table, sending it rolling. Dr. Perrin, fortunately, missed the two chairs.

Mari had been sitting at her small table and was enraged that I had landed in her home. But I had too much to do to be concerned with Mari's anger. She looked between me and the two prone forms on the floor, appearing to recognize Vadim in his glamour suit.

"Arcanimus have left. There was a poisonous gas in the basement and the place is trip wired for magic. Can you see to Vadim, I need to help the Doctor." Mari remained stern for a second longer then capitulated. She wasn't a stupid or mean woman and there was a wounded man in front of her.

As I tried to get Dr. Perrin into a more comfortable position, I realized that Vadim was still in his glamour suit. I reached across the small space and peeled it off his head, dislodging the mask at the same time. He couldn't be properly treated with the glamour obscuring his body.

"Ahhhhh," gasped Mari. "This isn't Tola's son?"

I answered yes quickly and went back to Dr. Perrin. It struck me as curious that Mari would recognize Vadim through his mother, but it was a piece of information for later. Now there were more pressing concerns.

Dr. Perrin was just barely breathing. It came in short, wispy gasps. I loosened her clothing, hoping to help her breathe. I sucked in my own breath sharply when I saw the black bruise forming across Dr. Perrin's chest. She'd been struck with an killing blast—an invasive fireball of poison that is only used to kill.

"Hold on Dr. Perrin. Hold on." I took the Doctor's hand and rubbed it vigorously then laid it pressed against my chest. My other hand I placed on Dr. Perrin's wound.

"Hold on now, Miss. You'll take on her hurt if you do that." Mari rose to her feet and dug through a nearby dresser. She came back with a large smoky quartz. "Put that between your hand and her wound."

I did as I was told and began the quiet breathing that heralded the complex healing spell I was about to try. I had never been good at healing spells. They took time and patience to learn, practice, and administer, but I knew the theory and at that moment I was willing to do anything to save Dr. Perrin.

Once I started pulling the pieces of the spell together in my mind I sent it down through the hand resting on my chest. A flicker of gold ran the length of Dr. Perrin's arm. At the same time, I began pulling on the magic in the wound through the crystal. I could feel the spell lurking there, evil and dull. With my mind, I plucked at it, pulling bits and pieces off of it and into the smoky quartz.

With the last of the gold healing spell traveling into Dr. Perrin, I made a mighty effort and pulled hard on the spelled wound, but only a portion of it came out.

I released Dr. Perrin and fell back. The effort of trying to heal had exhausted me. And as I tried to catch my own breath, I heard Dr. Perrin's breath become more rapid and feverous. I sprang to the doctor's side, grasping her hand.

"Dr. Perrin, can you hear me. Dr. Perrin wake up. We can help you if you can just open your eyes a bit." I was pouring my strength into the dying woman. I started to waver from the effort, but then strengthened with renewed energy when I felt a large hand and a small, bony hand laid upon my back. Vadim was awake and lending me his strength, as was the medium Mari.

"Esme is that you? Is that little Esme?" Dr. Perrin choked out.

"It's me Dr. Perrin. I've come to rescue you. What did they do to you? Tell me so I know how to fix you." I spoke quietly, yet desperately.

Dr. Perrin moved her head slightly as if to wave off the silly idea. "Cannot." She rasped. "You must stop them." She was quiet again for a moment. I didn't dare breathe for fear I would miss what Dr. Perrin would say next.

"In space, communi...cation satellite. Beam enhancer so can increase magic power, even in air."

"But how Doctor, how?" I smoothed Dr. Perrin's forehead, still holding her hand closely. The doctor remained quiet for so long, I despaired of losing her before we could get the information. To lose the Doctor would be a tremendous tragedy. To have her die in vain would be worse.

"Stole my enhancer. Still need a power source. Self-generating, won't fail in air, space." Dr. Perrin tried to lean up to cough. I caught her head and lifted her a little. "Couldn't make a power source, didn't need me now." She lay panting, her head now cradled in my lap. Tears were welling in my eyes. I knew I couldn't help her much more.

A slow minute ticked by. Dr. Perrin looked to be struggling for breath. Then with all the effort of her will, she pulled her hand from mine and let it land over her breast pocket. "Here, inside."

I carefully reached into the inner pocket of Dr. Perrin's lab coat and pulled out a piece of scratch paper, badly folded. I opened it with one hand finding a carefully written diagram of a machine.

"Enhancer," Dr. Perrin's voice came out in a whisper of air. "Don't let them get it to space. Bad results." She gasped a long breath. I took her hand again trying to send every last bit of healing spell into the broken woman.

"Please hang on. Just hang on." I felt the slightest of squeezes on her hand. Dr. Perrin opened her eyes once more, giving me a slight, far away smile, then she let out a long, soft breath and was gone.

I didn't realize I was crying until I felt Vadim's arms around me. He quietly pulled me away from the Dr. Perrin's body. I sobbed uncontrollably. After a few minutes, Vadim succeeded in quieting me down. He wiped my face with Hakim's robe. Mari had busied herself by arranging the body and covering it with a blanket.

"Better now?"

"I'm sorry. I shouldn't have lost control like that." I pulled away from the kneeling Vadim noticing for the first time that he was naked from the waist up. From the waist down he was still in his glamour suit. I giggled hysterically for a second, pointing down to the suit. I took a great gulp of air to calm myself. "We need to get a team here to investigate."

Vadim was wriggling out of the rest of his suit. Mari stood up.

"This is what I get for trying to stop those stupid Arcanimus. If you bring in an investigating team, the Daughters of Islam will be all over me." Mari starting collecting items from around the room, placing them in a bag. Mumbling to herself I continued, "Ridiculous state magic agencies. As if a bureaucrat gets witchcraft. Silly, silly."

She found her crystal ball in a corner and sat with it in her lap for a moment. Vadim was calling for clothing, as he had only his underwear on. I tried to erase the evidence of my emotional breakdown using a small mirror hanging on the wall, but my nose was just too red to do anything about.

Mari left the room and came right back in bearing the shingle that had hung outside her door, indicating her services. She leaned it against the wall. She took up her bag and handed me the crystal ball. "I'll be off now," I made to protest but Mari put up her hand to shush me, "Its all there in the glass, everything I've seen. I don't want to be bothered with investigators. Do what you must." In a flash, Mari had taken a leap from the room.

Vadim and I looked at each other across the dimly lit room, then at the crystal ball.

"Call Mistress, let her organize the investigation. It will have to be multi-national. This is going to take more than just AMIS."

I nodded and took my compact from my pocket. "Mistress," I said as I opened it up, "Agent O'Rourke reporting in."

It took a few minutes before Mistress answered. It looked as if I had woken her, she was a bit groggy. I quickly explained the situation and Mistress was up to her usual speed.

"I want a full report, in my office, in the next half hour. Bring Vadim with you. I'd like to see that boy again. I'll send Stanford and Harker to secure the area. Once they arrive, come to me."

Chapter 9

Washington, DC

June 24, 1959

Vadim and I jumped straight to Washington once the containment agents arrived. Vadim didn't protest, so I didn't ask why he didn't check in with his own agency. He had every right to want a co-agency investigation. After all, he was an enemy agent—even in these uncertain times. Yet he was going along as if it were really my call.

As soon as we walked through Mistress's office door, she stood up, to her full height of five feet two, and hobbled over to Vadim leaning heavily on her cane.

"Vadim, my boy! It does me good to see you after so long a time," Mistress held out her arms for an embrace. I felt a bit of envy mixed with distrust as Vadim leaned in for a kiss on his cheek. I had never got such a warm welcome from Mistress, even when I didn't mess up.

"Now, now," said Mistress smiling naughtily as she made her way back to her seat, "back to business."

As she resumed her chair, she resumed her habitual straight face. "Esmeralda, please report in full."

As I assumed my report-giving stance, I couldn't help but notice the smirk on Vadim's face. It was just like being a teenager again with him around. Always having to check in with Mistress. Always having to apologize for trouble-making. I was more than 30 now, I really should be able to not get into these humiliating situations anymore.

"Ma'am," I began and in a few short minutes gave a quick, yet full, sketch of the events of the past 40 hours.

"Thank you, Agent. You have the crystal ball with you now." Vadim unslung his pack and removed the ball. He handed it to Mistress. "My dear Vadim, would you please inform me of your involvement in this inquiry."

Vadim, like I, made his statement quickly and professionally. And he took my sneer with as much grace as I had taken his.

"I have called a special meeting at the UN for an intramagic service security meeting. It will meet at sixteen hundred hours. Right now, why don't you both get some rest and I'll wake you in enough time to debrief you both. Esmeralda, please show our guest to the rest area." Mistress gave me a sharp once over. "Perhaps you might visit the healer. You are looking worse for wear."

I nodded and left. Vadim following closely. As I walked silently down the long corridors to the staff lounge areas, I began to feel the fatigue of the events getting to me. After showing Vadim to a room he could use. I took a hot shower and fell asleep almost instantly.

Mistress sent Agent McMann to wake me. It seemed like no time at all had passed, but the clock read that is was past seven am. I went to wake Vadim myself. He was deeply asleep, with one arm thrown over his face. I had to shake him to wake him, but when he did he was instantly alert and ready to go.

Agent McMann had informed me that Mistress wanted us in her office. After some quick morning ablutions, Vadim and I headed down the labyrinthine halls to Mistress's office. I was barely awake and having trouble stifling my yawns. Once there, we found a table laid for a meal.

"I took the liberty of ordering breakfast for you both. I know you must be hungry." I fumed, becoming wide awake instantly. I knew that Mistress was showing off for Vadim, but that didn't make his prince-like treatment any less appalling. "There now, we can talk plans while we eat."

Mistress's personal assistant, Virginia, came through the door that connected their offices wheeling a food trolley with covered dishes on top. Apparently she was meant to be waitress. Virginia was about 45 and had worked for mistress for years. She was the daughter of a witch, but held very little magic herself. She could only work fire and maybe a small bit of levitation, but she was good-natured and put up with Mistress's taciturn moods better than any one else ever would.

Virginia uncovered the dishes revealing a complete breakfast of eggs, bacon, pancakes and juice.

"Ah! an American-style meal. I haven't eaten this in years." Vadim said enthusiastically.

Virginia began serving the food. Once her back was turned on Mistress, she looked at Vadim and then gave me a wink.

I tried not to blush, but wasn't so successful. Fortunately Vadim and Mistress were speaking and took no notice.

Everyone in the agency knew about me and Vadim, knew our complete history. Sometimes I wished I could have a job in a place where no one knew the intimate details of my whole life. It had been years since I had last had contact with Vadim, as everyone knew. And everyone also knew how badly our relationship had ended.

But it had been more than a decade since we had gone our separate ways. I shouldn't have to undergo this scrutiny from my fellow agents. After all, it had been Vadim that had left. He should be getting the knowing winks. But he didn't because no one knew how he took our falling apart. Any agent in service before 1950 knew how I took it—badly.

I was young then, just twenty, and the love of my life decided to join the service of KGBB, thereby severing any possible relationship we could ever have.

Vadim was half Russian and half Polish, even after the USSR annexed Poland, he could have gone to any Western country and found a place in their service. Yet, he swore service to KGBB. They had promised him news of the whereabouts of his mother. She had disappeared during the Soviet invasion of Hungary, near the time of the fall of Budapest in 1945, those last few months of the European war.

I never knew if KGBB actually had information about his mother or had just lied to him in order to recruit him. I believed it was the latter. I would have heard in the intervening years if Tola were still alive, or even if she was dead. My mother had searched for her friend for years. And Mistress would have passed along any information she received, knowing how personally involved I was, yet there had been no news, nothing. Vadim had thrown our life together away for an untruth.

Whether or not he wanted to return to me, I knew there was no chance of it. Once swearing loyalty to KGBB, an agent would die before betraying them, literally. Their oath of fealty was magic bound with a deadly curse. Break the oath and die.

I knew it had been a hard decision for him to make, but it still hurt. Even though I knew he had to do it. I would have done the same thing. But all these years later it still hurt as it did the day he left.

Mistress unceremoniously called me to attention by tapping me on the shoulder with her cane. "Will you pay attention, girl."

"I'm sorry, what?" I replied lamely. I found I had a full plate of great smelling food. Mistress and Vadim were already well into their meal and Virginia was no where to be seen.

"Please eat already, or are you still too tired?"

"I'm fine." I dug into my food with enthusiasm.

"I was just telling Vadim that I spoke with Comrade Ignatievich, the director of KGBB," said Mistress eyeing me shrewdly. "I spoke with Comrade Ignatievich and he agreed to send in their special curse cracking team to Damascus to take care of the Arcanimus safe house."

"Comrade Vasha is the best. He'll take care of the job in no time."

"Wonderful, wonderful." Mistress took a small, elegant bite of egg. After chewing thoughtfully, she began again. "I have gotten full approval from Boris Ignatievich for the use of your services. It took only a little persuading."

Vadim and I grinned at each other like we were kids again.

"I believe that once we have decided on a path to follow, I will send you two along on assignment. I will attend to the security meeting myself. This plot of those ridiculous Arcanimus people really takes precedence over everything else." Again she had a small bite. "Yet I've got two requests from the State department for special surveillance and a coven of witches in the Midwest that need investigating, let alone our normal investigations. This is most distracting."

Vadim and I continued to plow through our meal. Mistress liked to dominate any conversation and I think we were both too hungry to even attempt to interrupt her.

"Now, from what I gather, the Arcanimus have developed a machine that can broadcast magic from space, thereby enhancing the use of magic on earth." Mistress made a face indicating her distaste. "The machine is embedded in a communications satellite, I believe that is the technology of which we are speaking, which will allow for use of magic while not based on land."

It was common knowledge that in the air, magic became tricky and hard to control. Strong witches never flew in aircraft for fear of bringing it down. Magic worked better on or under water, but for full use and mastery, it was best to practice magic while sure footed on earth.

"Dr. Perrin, god rest her soul, said that the only remaining obstacle for putting the machine into use was a self-renewing power source." Both Vadim and I had finished our meal while Mistress spoke. She took another slow bite. "I have been considering this problem. I'm sure Dr. Perrin thought of it and did not mention it, but the only source of magic that is a source in itself is Saturn stone. As I'm sure you know, it is very rare and only found in small pieces—most no bigger than this potato here." She stabbed a piece of roasted diced potato. "It would take a huge sized rock and probably quite a number of smaller pieces to create the kind of energy that would make it work in outer space."

"I've never seen a Saturn rock before Mistress. What does it look like?" Vadim asked.

Mistress pulled a long gold chain from her coat pocket and draped it across the salt shaker in the middle of the table. The long chain held a oval pendant. Set in gold was a large shiny stone about four inches long by two wide and an inch thick. The stone was wonderful to watch. It held a myriad of colors which changed and flashed as it twinkled from the overhead lighting, but it didn't seem to be of any color at all.

"It's beautiful," Vadim said quietly.

"Try picking it up." I had held it once before and knew what to expect when Vadim reached his hand out for it. At first he jerked his hand back, then grasping it all the hairs on his arm stood on end. His face looked shocked then pleasantly surprised. I watched as all the hair on his head stood up as well. Another second longer and he was back to normal.

"Amazing!" he cried.

"That is the largest piece that is commonly known to exist. Quite remarkable isn't it? Yet a hundred such pieces as that would not be enough to sustain magic in the void of space. Do you see what I'm getting at?"

"Yes, I do."

"So unless those Arcanimus devils have devised a spell-based renewable energy source—which I highly doubt since witches much more talented than those fools have never been able to develop one—Saturn stone will be their best hope."

"If it doesn't exist, it doesn't exist. I don't see where this is leading." I finally put in.

"It may exist, my dear, that is the problem. Just because we do not know of it, doesn't mean it couldn't exist."

"Okay, then what is your plan?"

"I want the two of you to go to the Laksanika Oracle and consult with the sage-on-duty. Perhaps she will be able to tell us the information we seek. Knowing Himiko, she will have thought of seeking advice there as well. We also need to know if she or any of her followers have been there. I want you to go as soon as we are finished here."

"Great! Let's go now," I made to get up from the table.

"Not yet," Mistress scolded. "I have not finished my breakfast. Don't be rude."

I sat back down silently, holding back my extreme urge to roll my eyes. Mistress continued her meal at a leisurely pace.

"Esme dear, do you still have the mirror necklace I had you wear as a child?"

"Of course." When I was under Mistress's care, I always had to wear a communication mirror around my neck. That way Mistress could more easily monitor my whereabouts.

"I think you should wear that for the next few days so we can be in close contact. Things might get a bit hairy and it could come in handy."

I nodded. The last thing I wanted was to be monitored like a child again. Especially in front of Vadim. He would think that nothing had changed between me and Mistress. Granted not a whole lot had changed, but I did spend much of my time taking care of myself these days.

"Once you've met with the sage-on-duty and consulted the oracle, I need you to come straight back here. No side trips," she eyed us both sternly. "If I'm not back from the Security Council meeting, wait for me. From there we will decide our next path of inquiry."

With that, Mistress pushed herself away from the table, placed her napkin neatly beside her plate and stood up. "Please hurry on this matter. As you know, it is of the upmost importance."

Chapter 10

Peak of Dhobertali, Village of Solang, Himachal Pradesh, Northern India

June 25, 1959

The first thing that I felt when I landed on the entrance platform was the icy wind. It was blowing fiercely and before I got my feet firmly planted, it threatened to blow me off the narrow wedge of decking stuck in the mountain peak. It didn't help that the landing stage was covered with snow. Vadim appeared a split second after me and was caught so off guard, I had to catch him by the arm before he tumbled off.

Once we were both steady we moved closer to the small post made out of rock, sticking out of the snow by about two feet. The sun was just going down across the edge of the mountain range, casting the whole panorama of mountain caps in a lovely golden light. I would have loved to have waited to watch the sun dip beyond the farthest peak, but it was piercingly cold and I had not dressed for the weather.

I crouched in front of the rock post and casted a spell of entry and opening. It came out as a little globe of light, much the same color as the sunset. I placed it over the post and waited, holding my elbows trying to keep in my warmth. Before I could count to ten, the post disappeared beneath the snow leaving a gaping dark hole. Both Vadim and I leaned over to pear down the hole when it opened up wide, revealing a long staircase.

"I guess we are welcomed by the Sage-on-duty." I said as I took a tentative step down to the first stair.

"For some reason she must think its safe to let you pass." I could hear the taunt in Vadim's voice. He teased me to start an argument so that he could laugh when I got mad. I knew what he was trying to do, yet it was still so hard to resist.

The staircase was very old and carved out of the mountain granite and dirt. It wasn't supported with any form of construction, but I could see that the walls and stairs were very sturdy. I had never been to visit the Laksanika Oracle before, but had been fascinated by it as a kid.

The Laksanika Oracle was thousands of years old. No one knew who established the oracle or why, but since around the sixth century, a clan of witches had been the caretakers. For the first few centuries, it had been limited to clan of witches from the Tibetan Plateau, but in later centuries had grown to encompass much of the northern part of the subcontinent of India. Each witch in the clan had to spend a year on the mountain as the caretaker of the Oracle to be considered of age. The year was meant to encourage young witches to get in touch with their magic, to really learn it and its uses.

It seemed like a long way down the dark stairs, but I found myself becoming more and more excited by the chance to meet one of these young sages. I knew I could never stay put for a year by myself on the mountainside, but I had tremendous respect for these young witches who did.

Finally reaching the bottom of the stairs, there was a humble wooden door. Not really knowing if I should knock or just go in, I decided to just go in.

I found myself in a brightly lit, spacious room. On my left was a girl talking to someone else in a hand mirror. When she realized she had guests, she hastily said goodby and placed the mirror face down. She got up, quickly rearranging her sari and scarves.

"You got here quickly, it takes most people at least five minutes longer, not that many people come by that door." She spoke quickly, and petulantly, in Hindi.

Vadim and I had been prepared for the language and had cast the language spells on each other.

"Thank you for admitting us," Vadim said politely.

"My pleasure," said the girl. She was about 15 and very pretty with the large dark eyes that many Indian women had. She smiled brightly at Vadim with a sauciness that would give any American bobby-soxer a run for their money. I arched an eyebrow and looked around the room. It was a glorified studio apartment—a small cooking area, a bath area, a corner for bedding and clothes, with a large fireplace at the opposite side. I was furthered dismayed to see a radio cabinet with a record player and a large number of records. Near the bed were several posters of Indian singers and actors, including Dilip Kumar and Nargis.

"Just another teenager," I thought, not without a little disappointment.

Vadim introduced himself and me and told the girl we were there to consult with the Oracle.

"Of course you are," said the girl. "My name is Latika, the current Sage-On-Duty. Pleased to be of service." She bowed her head very low. "Please come in and stay awhile. I get so dreadfully bored here all by myself. Not to mention all the pilgrims this time of year." She sighed.

"Pilgrims?" asked Vadim.

"All those Hippies come here, come to the holy mountain to see the hermit. It's such a dreadful bother."

"You have to be the hermit as well?" I prompted.

"Oh yes. Who wants to look like a skinny old man in rags?" Latika absentmindedly drew out the silk of her sari and let it fall. "Only, one of the guides from the village is in on this secret. His mother is part of the clan. Its fun when he brings the pilgrims for he tells them I'm saying the funniest things. Its hard to keep from laughing in front of them. And the pilgrims take him so seriously!"

"You said that not many come by the entrance we used. I thought witches came all the time to visit the Oracle." I innocently asked, taking advantage of the girl's talkative nature.

"Hardly anyone comes that way." Latika replied earnestly. "My mother visits every week," she made a face that let it be understood that she really didn't consider her mother to be anyone special. "I took over at the new moon in February, and there has only been one old lady who came and that was months ago."

"Oh, it must be boring for you." Vadim piped in. I was pleased to know that no witches had been there recently.

"Very much," she said looking like she was very pleased to get to look at him again. "What did you need to ask the Oracle..."

Just then the large mantle piece, which looked like a large rock, set into the wall above the fireplace began to glow brightly. "Oh dear," Latika continued, "Pilgrims are arriving. I've got to go." She snapped her fingers and was instantly covered in a glamour that made her look like a wizened yogi. She hobbled to the side of the fireplace where there was a seam in the wall that was really a doorway into the main cave of the Oracle.

Curious, I cast a quick invisibility glamour over myself and followed Latika. Vadim just shook his head and sat on a cushion near the low table.

On the other side of the doorway, I saw a large cave that was lit by a torch on either side. Latika sat in a meditative pose in front of a beautiful alter. The altar was carved from a dark, smooth stone. Atop it was the same large rock that was the mantle piece of the fireplace behind. The rock on this side was framed by a miniature temple dedicated to Ushas, the Vedic goddess of dawn.

The pilgrims entered the entrance of the cave following a guide–a young man who looked liked like a local. The pilgrims were all European looking. There were a half dozen of them, but I had no time for them. I ducked back into the other room, discarding my invisibility in the process. I went over to examine the stone above the fireplace. The fireplace was not a fireplace but part of the altar in the cave on the other side. The stone, which I realized was the Oracle, seeming to glow with its own energy, was set into the cave wall, or was carved from it. I couldn't tell.

Examining the structure of the wall closely, I realized that everything about the wall and the altar was just one piece, all carved from the same stone. The Oracle stone was of a different material and obviously set into the carved wall. It was more than a foot high and about nine inches wide. From the angle, I couldn't tell how big around it wa.

Vadim watched me do what I did best–be curious. He watched me feel around the whole wall. Finally I spoke up.

"Do you remember that no one knows what the Oracle is really?" I didn't turn from examining the structure. "It is thought that it is the result of a powerful spell by a large group of exceptional witches. Although, there have been theories that it is something innately magical."

I put my hand out to the Oracle stone itself, close, but not quite touching it. "Vadim come look closer." Vadim rose and joined me. As he put his hand out next to mine, I said, "Are you thinking what I'm thinking?"

Vadim visibly gulped before he turned to look at me. "It's a Saturn stone." We stared at each other silently as the information sank in. This was just the thing that Himiko would need to operate her machine.

Vadim was first to break the silence, "But would Himiko figure it out?"

"If I were really trying to find a power source, I would. It only took you and I a quarter of an hour to figure it out and we weren't looking for it." I took a deep breath and looked back at the Oracle. "Even if she doesn't realize the Oracle is a Saturn stone, she will know that this is a source of magic that renews itself. Its been operating continuously for thousands of years."

"We should contact Mistress and get a guard set up." Vadim pointed at the delicate necklace around my throat. A star shaped pendent the size of a quarter hung from the chain. The flip side held a small mirror.

"Yes, that's a good idea." I said, absently clutching at the pendent. An old habit I developed to keep Mistress from overhearing anything. "However, I think we need to consult first with Latika. I think the guardians of the Oracle have been guarding a much larger secret than any of us ever knew."

"I think you're right."

"I also think that Mistress knew what we would find when she sent us here."

Vadim sat down again, placing his elbows on the table and his hands under his chin in a contemplative pose. I stared at the Oracle for a few minutes longer before turning back to Vadim.

"I wonder how much longer Latika will be with the pilgrims." Vadim shrugged. "I don't think she'll mind if I make some tea while we wait, do you?"

"I shouldn't think so."

Filling an earthenware tea pot from a water basin next to the small stove, Vadim snapped my fingers around the pot several times in succession. He opened the lid, steam rising, and threw in a pinch of tea he found in a container on the shelf above. Bringing the teapot and cups, he sat at the low table. I joined him, finally giving up my examination of the stone.

In a few minutes Latika, again in her brightly colored sari, joined us. She had a cup of the tea and entertained us for a few minutes with tales of the ridiculous pilgrims.

"I know that my year here is an honor, but sometimes it feels more like a punishment, especially when I have to work the oracle for visitors that have no idea what is really going on." The teenager leaned over the table, sighing deeply and dramatically.

"Latika," I began after a look of encouragement from Vadim. "I want to tell you why we are here. It is important, but I think it may be even more important than we even knew."

Latika settled her large dark eyes on me, my face a serious reflection of hers.

"The Arcanimus have developed a plan to launch an artificial satellite into space that will enhance the ability to wield magic of anyone who can. It could make very weak magic users quite capable and someone like the leader of Arcanimus invincible."

"Really," Latika answered with teenage scepticism.

"I know it sounds crazy, but if you hadn't realized it, both Vadim and myself are with agencies on a joint investigation into the Arcanimus's plans."

"Which agencies?"

"I'm with AMIS and Vadim is with KGBB." Latika looked at me and then Vadim her eyes growing wide with surprise.

"Is this true," she asked Vadim. In response Vadim reached out his left arm, turn his palm face up. There, scrolling across the lifeline of his palm, was his oath of fealty.

Latika gasped. "You guys are working together? It must be really important then."

"Its very important, Latika."

"But what have I got to do with it?" she asked.

"We were sent here to ask the Oracle, but only closer examination, we think that the Oracle itself maybe our answer."

Latika looked confused. "How do you mean?" Just then Oracle began to glow. Latika looked at it sharply. "People are coming in by the mountain gate. At least three. That is as many as the Oracle will count."

"There are more visitors coming from the landing on the peak," she continued quietly. In unison, I and Vadim stood and moved towards the far door.

"How long until they reach the bottom?" Vadim asked Latika who was looking a bit bewildered by their sudden movements.

"Usually seven to ten minutes. You both made it in less than that, so maybe four minutes at the earliest." Latika looked around the room, "What should I do?"

"Stay out of the way until we determine who the visitors are," I answered. Latika moved to the corner on the far side of the altar.

"Less than three minutes," I stated, looking at my watch. I began a stunning spell that I held concentrated in my upturned palm. Vadim was mouthing a chant with his ear to the door. I figured he was enhancing his hearing. Sooner than expected, Vadim closed his mouth and nodded at me. We each stood to one side of the door.

In a few seconds more, I could hear the movement on the other side of the door as well. The quiet was broken by a scream of warning from Latika, "Look out!"

It was too late. By the time I had turned to look back, a binding net was already sailing my way. I just had time to launch my stunning spell before it hit, binding my magic as well as my body. I hit the floor hard. A corresponding thump followed just after I landed, and I knew they had stopped Vadim as well.

The door behind us opened. I tried to crane my head to see who had come in, but the net was too well bound and I had no freedom of movement.

"Hello my dear friends," came a greeting in English from a well-known voice. A second later, I got a glimpse of Himiko as she leaned over my prostrate form. The corners of Himiko's mouth curved slightly. For Himiko, it was a huge show of emotion. "I saw you both enter from the peak entrance and would have been here sooner except that we didn't want to meet any of the pilgrims.

Himiko looked scornful "You didn't consider guarding the pilgrims entrance did you? I had my colleagues jump to the entrance, bypassing the sensor farther down the trail. That was an amateur mistake, I believe. Neither of you are amateurs, I know for a fact. I realized too late that it must have been you both who sneaked past my perimeter guards in Damascus. You were always very talented at getting to places you were not welcome."

I heard scuffling and the muffled cries of Latika. Powerless to do anything, my anger mounted.

"Don't be so rough with the girl. She's scared, but harmless." The scuffling stopped. The only sound in the room was Latika's sobbing.

"Work on removing the stone." Himiko commanded. More people came into the room from the upper passage, but I couldn't see anything except an occasional shoe.

Himiko continued to give instructions to her crew. I heard a long whining noise that was probably the result of a spell. Then the room became very hot and Latika's sobs became louder until she called out, "Please, please don't take it. Please, I beg you."

Her pleas, as far as I knew, were ignored. A few minutes later there was a loud sound of rock cracking, then the air in the room became smoky and dusty. I couldn't help myself from coughing.

Himiko had the Oracle stone placed in some sort of container. I heard the lid being fitted on and secured. Then I found I was looking at Himiko's feet.

"What to do with you two?" she mused aloud. She was enjoying the situation.

"I think you must know quite a bit to have made it here before me. Therefore, I think you both will have to come as my captives. You will travel better asleep."

That was the last thing I heard before I blacked out.

Chapter 11

Unknown

Unknown

My first feeling upon waking was a dull, cold ache down my right side. I opened my eyes to near complete darkness. I realized soon enough that I was lying, trussed up, on my side on stone or tile flooring. My hands were bound under my knees, so I was lying in a forced fetal position.

Once I had taken in as much of my surroundings as I could, I levered myself up to a sitting position with my elbow and some rocking. After that I simply pulled my hands under my feet. My hands were still bound but at least I could stretch and stand. I attempted to conjure a light. Nothing. The straps that bound my hands also bound my magic. I pulled at the leather-like material, but the straps didn't slip at all.

I was in a room made from, or carved from, stone. The room was much longer than it was deep and was dimly lit by the rectangle of light that shone around what must be the door. I walked to the door and felt around for a handle or pulley. I found nothing, not even hinges. The door was shut in place with magic and probably the slightest of barrier spells. I frowned in frustration. I gave the door a swift kick. I felt around the walls of the small room searching for some sort of gap or crack or hidden passage, but I found nothing.

I sank to the floor next to the door in a sulk. "Captured by Himiko, the Arcanimus, how humiliating," I thought. Now I was stuck in some unknown prison for who knew how long and I didn't know what had happened to Vadim or Latika. Then a truly terrifying thought came to me: what if I had been unconscious for so many days that I had missed the launch?

I strained to try to recollect any memories since I was spelled unconscious, but nothing was coming to me. "Vadim, where are you?" I said aloud to the dark, stone room. I would have been very close to despair, but I refused to be the type that gave in to the blues. I leaned my head back against the wall to consider every possibility. Once I was quiet, I thought I could hear the scrapings of footsteps nearby. I put my ear closer to the door in order to hear better. The steps grew closer.

All of a sudden the door was gone and Vadim came tripping through the door way, obviously pushed by his usher. A tall, dark woman appeared in the doorway and looked around the room. Finding me on the floor, she smiled broadly. Stepping back through the doorway she said in German, "Good you're awake. I'll take you to the boss."

I had been trying to worm myself into a position to launch myself at the guard. Just as I got to my knees, I was forced to stand upright so tall my feet were practically dangling below me. I just managed to call out as I was hoisted to the door, "You alright?"

Vadim answered with a mocking laugh, "Himiko never changes." The doorway was once again sealed by a door. I was forced to stumble on my tiptoes ahead of the malicious guard through a maze of dimly lit corridors. I was trying to memorize my way so that I could make it back for Vadim once I had freed myself, but as we walked on, I had the sinking feeling the guard was taking me in circles on purpose. Still I did chance to glimpse into some rooms as I passed and saw barracks, storage rooms, and a community room with a number of Arcanimus agents sitting at a table. I never saw a door or window to the outside, so I still couldn't name the time of day, even if it were day or night. I found that unnerving.

After walking for about seven minutes we came to a doorway, the guard knocked twice then opened it up. Inside was an office that was more furnished than any I had seen on my brief walk. There was carpeting and wall hangings, a lovely large cherry wood desk, and overstuffed chairs settled before a roaring fireplace. It looked quite cosy.

Himiko stood up from one of the chairs by the fireplace. "Wonderful, I'm glad you've finally woken." She gestured for me to sit in the chair opposite her. "I'm sorry you were unconscious for so long. I believe you must have taken the lion's share of the sleeping spell I sprung on you and Vadim. He woke up about 6 hours ago."

I did my best to settle in the chair and look comfortable, even though my hands were still bound together. "How long have I been out?"

"Since the Oracle's cave? Let's see," She consulted an antique baroque clock on the mantle above the fireplace. I examined her closely while she looked away. Himiko looked only slightly older. She'd lost the roundness in her face, but her dark eyes, if anything, were sharper and even more keen. "Just over 34 hours," Himiko replied.

I did some quick calculations. That would make it about 4 in the afternoon on June 26th in the U.S. There were still about time before the satellite launched.

"You didn't harm the girl?'

"The sage-on-duty? No. We left her there." Himiko sat comfortably in her chair staring straight into my face.

"What do you want with us?"

Himiko gave a small artificial sigh. "Must you be so straightforward? I thought we might catch up a bit first."

"Oh please, like we don't know everything about each other anyway." I said condescendingly. Himiko always had been like a little sister. "You have spies, I am a spy. Knowing about each other is what we do."

Himiko frowned. In that look, I could see the petulant teenager I once had known so well. Some things never do change, I thought. An unwilling grin surfaced on my face. At first Himiko was ready to fly into a rage, but she knew what the smile meant. I think, when we were kids, after I had freed her from her prison, she had idolized me, her rescuer from those dark years, her mentor in the mundane world afterwards.

We stared at each fiercely for a full minute before Himiko decided to answer me.

"You are correct. I do know about you. But what I don't know is this," a malicious look crossed her face, her eyes gleamed, "Do you love Vadim as much as ever."

Whatever I was expecting, I had not been prepared for that. "It doesn't matter how I feel. He works for the wrong side."

"The wrong side, or another side, like me?" I did not answer, I stared at the fire. Himiko did too.

"You know what I remember best about the years I spent with you both?" Himiko asked breaking the silence. "You both had been friends since childhood, you were deeply in love with one another, although neither of you knew it then, but you both made time for me. You and Vadim both treated me as an honored member of your club of two. It was the only time I ever felt like I had a family. You and Vadim were the siblings I never had."

We continued to look at the fire, steadily not looking at each other. I felt the same way about her, yet I wouldn't admit it. What we were nearly 14 years ago and what we were today were very different. We both had grown up reaching for different goals. Also, I would never admit it at that particular moment with my magic bound and Himiko as my captor.

"You can join me you know. Project Iris is my masterpiece." She looked at the fire then turned her sharp eyes back to me. "Iris was the messenger, in Greek mythology. So I have named our satellite Iris. It will be the messenger to the whole world that the time of magic has come."

I couldn't help but roll my eyes. "So dramatic."

Himiko ignored me. "Once the satellite is in orbit, things will change."

"What things?"

"We won't have to hide what we are anymore. Magic will be so enhanced that there will be no reason to fear retaliation. No person," she said with a disdainful sneer, "will be able to harm any witch. It will be a new world. We will finally have control." Himiko's eyes took on a dreamy quality as she described the world she would make in only a few days time. "Whole countries will belong to us, the people with true power, not the politicized machinations of so-called democracies. The world will belong to us."

"So what." I said, annoyed. Himiko whipped around to look at me.

"So what? It's everything, can't you see that? No more hiding, no more cowtowing, no more acting as if I couldn't turn every last mundane into a frog if I wished."

"Just because it will belong to you doesn't mean you'll fit in any better you know. If you have to change the whole world just to feel like you belong, you never will."

"You just don't get it." Himiko sat back in her chair crossing her arms.

I laughed at her. "It's just like that time, right after you came to us, when you wanted that pretty yellow dress in Macy's and were going to jump in and take it, but Mother wouldn't let you. You made the same face then. It's the same thing now. You don't understand why you can't have everything you want if you have the ability to take it."

Himiko's face turned to stone. Her whole body straightened up, chin held high. If one were to read her body language it would clearly be saying, I am above this talk.

"It was worth killing Peter? It was worth killing Dr. Perrin?" Himiko eyed me stonily. "She was so kind to you when we brought you back. She showed you so much magic you couldn't have learned by yourself."

"Dr. Perrin was an unfortunate casualty. I never meant for her to die, but she would be so uncooperative." Himiko stared intently at the fire. "And you are wrong. She was not a kind woman to me. She was a focused woman. Magic was everything to her."

"Yet still, she wouldn't help you project magic onto the whole world." I smirked at Himiko. "I bet you thought you could lure her to joining you with the promise of stronger magic."

"I had hoped to," Himiko answered plainly. "But her vision was narrow. She couldn't see how much good it would do the world."

"Good?"

"No more wars, no more starvation. Let me use my gifts for everyone's benefit."

"I think you do not understand the nature of witches. Yes, you'll be more powerful, but so will everyone else. Do you really think that we'll all just come together and make you our leader?" I shook my head, "It doesn't work that way."

She waved a hand at me, brushing away my last statement. "This is beyond the point. Things will be different in a few days time. I offer you a chance to join me in making the new world. You and Vadim together." It was my turn to sulk.

"I know what you are thinking. You think he can never break his loyalty vow to KGBB without killing himself." Himiko paused for effect. I didn't bat an eyelash. "I can break the vow. I've put a lot of study and thought into it and I know I can break it."

I clinched my teeth, but I would not fall for the bait. "I can see how much you want it. I can feel it radiating off of you, the desire to have Vadim to yourself again." Himiko watched me, waiting for a reaction.

"No matter, you will have time to think upon it." Himiko rose. "You and Vadim shall remain here until the satellite is safely in orbit."

I stood too. "How, exactly, are you going to get a satellite into space?"

Himiko grinned broadly. "Very funny Esme. I know you to be far too clever to trust any specific information to you. However unlikely the chances of you escaping may be, I know that there is still a chance."

I got up and walked before Himiko. As I reached the door I felt the familiar feeling of being hoisted off my feet and Himiko guided me back the stone prison room.

Himiko opened the door. Once inside she dropped me unceremoniously.

"As your duration here will be of some days I will try to make it more comfortable." She snapped and two light sconces appeared on the wall. "Bedrolls," she called, then pointed at the floor. Two rolls of bedding landed in a poof on the floor. Himiko waved her hand along the left hand wall and two doors appeared. One a small square, the size of a cupboard. The second a full sized door. "Bathroom is the large door. Food will be delivered through the small one."

Vadim hadn't moved from his sitting position against the wall since we had come in. After falling to my knees, I had moved into a cross-legged seat. "You must be jealous as hell to watch me wield this magic." She smiled with satisfaction. "I'll come for you personally when everything is settled. I hope you both will think about my offer."

She turned to leave. I seriously considered diving for her legs, but without magic of my own there would be no way to subdue her. I would most likely end up a frog like some mundane that had crossed paths with Arcanimus.

Himiko stopped in the doorway and turned back. "For the record Vadim, she does still love you." With that parting thought, she sealed the doorway.

The stone room was still. Neither Vadim nor I dared break the silence. Himiko had ungraciously broken the taboo that we each had been dancing around since we had joined up together a few days before.

"What now?" I started after enough time seemed to have passed.

"First thing is first," Vadim added, "Turn this way and I'll have a go at your binds."

I turned towards him. "Do you really think Himiko would overlook tying our hands properly?" I held my wrists towards him.

"No, but we should try everything before we give up."

"Who said anything about giving up?"

Vadim felt all around my wrists, testing the bindings. When he had satisfied himself that they could not be broken, he let go. It was my turn to test his, but I had no luck either.

"Again, what now?"

Vadim didn't answer, instead he pulled me to him, putting his bound hands over my head to embrace me. I did not struggle.

"I've missed you everyday."

I took my time in responding. With my head pressed up against his chest I could hear his heartbeat. I never wanted to move again. Yet I did. "It was your choice."

"I know."

I lifted his arms over my head and moved away. "We don't have time for this. We have to figure out a way to get out of here."

"Until you come up with a clever solution, all we have is time."

"Did Himiko tell you where the satellite is to be launched from? All she said to me was that it would be in a few days." I redirected the conversation.

"She didn't even tell me that much."

"Any idea where we are?"

"None," he replied. I made a 'harumph' sort of sound and sat back on my heals, my head against my knees. Vadim stretched his legs out, his hands behind his head.

We were both lost in thought and remained quiet for some time. I unfolded one of the bedrolls and stretched out on the floor. After awhile, Vadim came over to sit nearer to me.

"Did Himiko ask you to join her as well?"

"Yes," I lay with my back to Vadim. I didn't turn.

"Did she tell you her plans for me?"

I turned now to face him, "Do you think its possible? Do you really think she could break the oath?"

It was Vadim's turn to look away. "I don't know. There haven't been ten witches in history as powerful as she is, but I still don't think she could." He paused. "Even if she could, I would be a hunted man for the rest of my life, like my father was. They don't let you leave just because you can."

"If only I really knew it was possible, we could make it work."

Vadim looked back down at me, "So you do still love me."

"I never said that."

"Yet you told Himiko."

"I told Himiko nothing."

Vadim smirked and I scowled. "Can we work on getting out of here now?"

I sat up and went to search the walls of the room again. I opened the door to the bathroom—little more than a hole in the ground and a basin of water. I frowned at it. The cupboard door opened to an empty cube surrounded by stone. I fanatically picked around the edges of the door, searching for a weak spot. Himiko had cast the spell for the door. It would hold indefinitely.

Vadim stayed in the same spot and watched as I nervously scoured the room. As before, I came up with nothing. I checked my pockets, awkwardly, to see if I had anything in them that could be of service, but my pockets had been cleaned out. I looked at Vadim.

"I've already looked and they even took my watch."

I sat next to him, worn out. Suddenly a bell sounded. We both looked all over the room, but neither could see a source, yet it sounded as if the bell was right there next to us. I dashed to the bathroom and threw open the door. Nothing. Opening the cabinet told a different story. Inside the formerly empty cabinet were two trays with steaming hot food on them and a large pitcher of drink.

"I guess its dinnertime, or perhaps time for breakfast." I pulled out a tray and handed it to Vadim. Taking the second one and the pitcher, we sat on the floor for a picnic-style meal.

Afterwards, I laid down on the bedding. Vadim tried to lay his next to mine, but I insisted he sleep elsewhere. He placed his in line with mine, so we could lie head-to-head. I was going to object, but felt this was not a battle I had the energy to continue.

I laid down on my back and stared up at the rough-hewn, stone ceiling. "Any idea what this place could be?" I asked.

"I thought at first it might be a castle of European origin, but the stones are cut so roughly, it doesn't seem likely." Vadim brushed his hands against the wall. "Perhaps some sort of fortified cave or temple?"

"I don't think it is a cave. The ceilings are too even. It must be quite large. Perhaps we are in the sub-foundation portion of an old building. But where?"

"My first guess was South Asia, in a temple complex."

"That makes sense. Perhaps Cambodia or Burma."

"While you were with Himiko, I examined the walls more thoroughly, I think we might be in a fortress in North Africa. The stones seem more like sandstone and the air is very dry. I think if we were in Cambodia we would still feel the effects of the humid conditions even in this rock complex."

"So if we figure out how to get in touch with our magic again. You think we should leap from North Africa?" I frowned. To properly teleport, one must know where one is and where one is going. There is an element of distance estimation in jumping from one place to another. Its not as if a witch literally figured out the distance with pencil and paper every time she moved about the world, but you did have to have a rather specific knowledge of geography. Unfortunately, North Africa was practically as big as all of Europe. Trying to do a specific jump would be rather risky.

"Well, we could try and find out where we are specifically." Vadim said a bit defensively.

After a pause, I said, "Remember that time I jumped you to Brazil?"

Vadim had laid down with his head just a foot away from mine. He chuckled at the memory. "You wanted to go to Brazil and didn't think where in Brazil. We must have landed at the very center."

"In the jungle," I laughed. "I just wanted to try the food in Rio."

"And you couldn't figure out where we were so we had to walk and jump our way across Brazil to find a town you knew." We were both laughing outright by this time.

"And none of our magic worked against the mosquitos. We were so dirty by the time we jumped back. Mistress had a fit." I laughed harder just remembering her lecture. I was so nervous then. Now I recognized it for what it was.

"You know, I collect local mosquito spells and charms now. I never want to be quite without the proper repellent magic again."

"You do not!" I expostulated. We were both laughing very hard. Vadim had turned onto his side to get some air. I had sat up, my arms around my knees, rocking with laughter. "We were so dumb!"

We laughed a few minutes more. When we both started to calm down, I added, "We couldn't have been more than 11 or 12. What idiots we were. You especially to just go with any stupid idea I had."

"Hey! I wasn't stupid, just in..." He stopped before finishing his sentence.

I turned and looked down at him. He had stopped laughing altogether. I laid down on my side, mirroring his pose, our heads nearly touching.

"Do you think we'll get out in time to stop her?" I asked quietly.

"I think so. I know you'll come up with something clever any minute now." Vadim reached his hands up and I did too. We tentatively held hands.

"Vadim," my voice was shaking, "Have you had girlfriends? Are you married? Have you been happy?"

He took a long time to answer me. Each of us immobile, hardly even breathing. "I have not been happy. As to girlfriends, well, not really. I can't trust anybody in my section and those are the women I meet most often. I tried to get to know a mundane woman or two, but I just didn't know how to talk them." He sighed. "I haven't been happy, no."

Having grown up with one another first in an opera company constantly on the move and then in Washington during war time, neither of us had ever really had a chance to get used to talking to normal people. We were always around people a lot older than us who were busy with their work. I found it as hard as he did.

I squeezed his hands. "I...," I meant to tell him about my dating experiences in the years we had been apart, but I just couldn't bring myself to say it aloud.

"I know about Martin Shermer in Copenhagen." Vadim filled in the information for me.

"Oh. You do."

"Anybody else?"

"Not really, no."

"What happened with Martin Shermer?" Martin was a brief fling for me. He was a son of a witch from Denmark and worked as an administrator in their magic bureau.

"He didn't like it that he could never pick me up in person. I always leapt to Copenhagen when we went out on a date.

He wanted me to move there, but I wouldn't. After that it just didn't seem like there was anything else to do."

"Have you been happy?"

"Happy enough. The memory charm helps."

"Do you wear that for me?"

I didn't answer him.

"I'm sorry," Vadim said. He pulled my hands to his face and kissed them. I let him.

"Tell me that you found out about your mother. Tell me that it was worth it."

Vadim was silent for some time. Neither of them were in a hurry for this conversation. "No," he finally whispered. "It was all a ruse. You were right."

"You've found out nothing about her in all these years?" I asked weakly.

"No, nothing. She disappeared. Like your mother."

We gripped each other's hands in comfort, in solidarity. Neither of us spoke again.

I must have fallen asleep for the next thing I knew the bell was going off again. Time for another meal.

Time passed this way for awhile. Meals would be served through the little cupboard set in the wall. Then the we would either sleep, talk, or exercise by doing calisthenics or sparring—both of which were very much hindered by our bound hands.

It was sometime after the ninth bell—I thought they were about twelve hours apart—we were sparring using our bedding as a mat. I had just maneuvered an elbow into Vadim's ribs when on my twist away he caught my arms and turned me over his back. I landed hard on my knees and elbows. "Damn it!" I cursed and then let my body slide to the floor. It felt good to stretch out on my stomach, not really having had a chance too since I had arrived there. With my hands bound, it wasn't an easy position to get into.

"Ouch!" I screamed and shot up. My hands to my chest.

"What is it?" Vadim was kneeling by my side in a half a second.

"Something just poked me," I answered. I patted around for a bit and then my eyes grew wide with excitement. "Vadim, I think its my mirror pendant."

"Huh?"

I stood up and turned my back to Vadim. I reached under my turtleneck and felt around in my bra and camisole until I found what had poked me. Deftly I plucked it out and brought my hands out.

"Look!" I showed Vadim my treasure. "It must have fallen off before Himiko's henchwomen searched me."

"We've been here for god knows how long and you just now discover that hidden in your..."

"How was I supposed to know? Its not as if I've had a chance to change my clothes since we've been here."

"First I wouldn't say it had fallen off, more like in." Vadim grinned at me, "Second, how could you not know a sharp pointy thing was in your under clothing all this time. And third, let's get Mistress on the horn now."

If I hadn't been so excited by my discovery I would have given him a swift kick—especially as he was still kneeling below me.

"Maybe we should break the mirror and use it to cut our way out. I really don't want to talk to Mistress right now. She is going to be very, very angry."

Vadim called me a chicken.

"Fine, we'll call Mistress."

I joined him on the floor and set the necklace charm between us. A communication mirror is spelled, so its magic is independent of the witch who uses it. I moved away from the charm and leaned over it. I didn't want to be too close to it on the off chance that the binding spell would radiate towards it.

"Mistress," I called. I waited a few seconds and then called again. Vadim looked at me and I looked at the mirror-side of the charm expectantly. After a few more seconds, a small sliver of Mistress's face resolved itself in the mirror.

"Where in the world have you two been?" she began indignantly. "Its been days since you were last supposed to check in.

And this note from Himiko herself telling me you had joined her side. Harumph!"

"Well," I began not knowing where I should start. "We haven't joined Himiko, but we are being kept prisoner by her. Where? I don't know. I only just now discovered that the mirror charm hadn't been removed when the Arcanimus striped us of our things."

"Are you magic bound?" I moved my hands over the mirror so that Mistress could see. "I'm going to work on a casting I can send through the mirror to break the binding. While I do, fill me in on your escapades."

So I told her the very few things that had happened since we had left her four days before.

"We know about the Oracle," Mistress responded when I was finished. "The mother of the current Sage-on-duty came to visit probably about 11 hours after you were taken. I always had my questions about the origins of the Oracle. I hate to have them answered at such a time and in such a way. However, I shall tell you what you need to know from this end."

At the Security meeting it was agreed that both the Soviet launch and the U.S. launch would have a uni-lateral security team searching for intruders. The Soviet launch was just about 3 and 1/2 hours ago. Thirty three minutes prior to launch, the Security team encountered two known Arcanimus agents and arrested them. "They are currently being interrogated and their parcel is being deconstructed. I need you to get there as soon as you can to see if you can find out if it was an actual attempt by Arcanimus or just a distraction. The security team for the U.S. launch has been called off since it is believed the plot has already been foiled," Mistress paused. "We all know that was too easy. My fear is the real plot will be carried out at Cape Canaveral. You need to get to Baikonur now and inter-rogate the prisoners yourselves. Now, put your hands out and keep them as far apart as you can."

I did as I was told. A bright blue spark slowly melted through the mirror and hovered between the mirror surface and my arms. "Now gently place the bonds into the spark."

I let my arms down slowly and with a ear-piercing whine, my restraints snapped into two and then shriveled to nothing. "Thanks," I told Mistress as I turned and stretched my wrists and hands.

"Sorry Vadim, but I must leave you in Esmeralda's hands. As soon as you are safe and know where you are, check in. I'll send a team in to secure the building as soon as I know where to send them."

I took the charm and secured it around my neck, this time double checking the clasp. I even went as far as to spell it secure. Then I turned to Vadim's restraints.

"I don't know what spell Mistress used, but I think I don't need to be so elaborate." Taking a deep breath I felt my connection to my magic restored. Placing my palms up in front of me, I focused until a small white glow appeared. Mouthing the quick release spell, the glow turned from a bright yellow to a sunset red. Then I let it go over Vadim's outstretched wrists. The red glow spread itself over the black of the bindings and before I could count to five it all disappeared.

"Let's go," said Vadim standing and heading towards the door. The door didn't stand a chance against Vadim. And before another thirty seconds was out, Vadim and I were in the dimly lit hallway. Vadim stopped short, looking from one direction to the other.

"Its this way," I pointed. "When Himiko brought me back, she brought me directly." I led the way.

We didn't see anybody for the first three-fourths of the way. Finally we heard voices coming up before us. Nearing the room the voices were coming from, the we slowed down. We realized it was the dining hall and that there were about eight Arcanimus within. They were apparently enjoying their meal because not one of them noticed when I quietly shut the door. Vadim was already sealing it shut, touching the four corners of the door. We moved on.

Near the room that was Himiko's, we found a guard. She had no chance between my invisibility glamour and Vadim's knock-out charm. About a hundred feet further down the corridor, we finally came to some stairs that only led up. I took point and sprinted up to the first landing. There was a door leading off each side, but the stairs continued up. When Vadim reached the landing, I dashed up the next flight. I found myself in an unguarded, short corridor with a window at each end. It was daylight. Early morning it looked like. Eyeing the corridor, I found there was a spiral staircase just next to the straight stair. There were two doorways on the opposite wall and one to the left down the corridor.

After Vadim reached the top, we hastily consulted. Our consensus was to take the stairs as far as we could go. At the top of the spiral case we found a large, round room with two guards.

"Lookout tower," I mouthed to Vadim. I pointed at the guard to the right and then to myself. The guard directly in front was Vadim's. He nodded.

Bursting into the room, we each stunned our opponent with hardly a flash of light. I bound my guard, using the magic binding net I found in the guards belt. I tossed Vadim an extra net and he bound his guard. Leaving the two women trussed up on the floor, we began searching the room for the identity of our prison.

The tower room had windows on all sides. Tentatively touching one, I found that it was a spelled window—not real glass. The whole place, as far as I could see was quarried from the same rock that had been my prison for the last few days. The building was perched on a cliff above a large body of water—an ocean or sea.

There were three desks lining the room with various instruments tumbling off of each one. I suspected they were some type of magic detection. I went to the nearest desk and began pulling out drawers. Odds and ends and leftover lunches filled the drawers. The same in the desk nearest Vadim. The third desk's drawers were identical to its neighbors, but this desk had a pull out panel—the kind used for extra desktop space. Glued to it was a map of the area, including the sea.

"I told you so." Vadim had been correct. We were on the coast of the Red Sea in Sudan.

"That's it," I pointed. I pulled out my charm necklace from below my turtleneck. "Mistress."

"It took you long enough to get out. Where are you."

I ignored her and turned the necklace to face the map. Turning it back over I said, "Once the assault team lands outside have them jump up to the lookout tower. We've bound the two guards. From there they go down the spiral staircase, turn right and take the straight stairs down."

"I believe we can handle it from here," was all that Mistress had to answer with. "You two, get going. Its only five hours until launch in Florida."

I turned to Vadim, "Ready?" He nodded and took my hand to teleport into the U.S.S.R.

Chapter 12

St. Petersburg and Baikanur Cosmodrome, U.S.S.R.

July 2, 1959

Since Vadim had control of the jump, I was surprised when we arrived in a small apartment. Looking around at the messy bed and rumpled clothing that littered the floor, I realized very quickly where we had jumped to.

"Why did we come to your apartment?" I demanded.

Vadim was already rummaging through his closet. I saw that it was just a small studio apartment with a hotplate for a kitchen. I knew there were always housing shortages in the Soviet Union, but this was too much. How could a key agent in KGBB be reduced to such meager living arrangements? Looking out the dirty window I saw a busy street about three stories below and a street lined with similar but drab looking six story buildings. Hardly any sunlight got beyond those high buildings.

"At least tell me what city this is?" I asked, less assertively.

Vadim pulled some clothes out from a pile in the bottom of his closet. "Stalingrad. We had to come here first. There is no way we'll get into the Cosmodrome, let alone be allowed to interrogate the prisoners unless we look the part." He tossed to me a dull brown dress uniform. "You know how the bureaucracy is. Believe me, its much easier to navigate if you look the part."

I held up the dress. It was at least five sizes too big for me. "Either your girlfriend is huge or you've been cross dressing again."

"Very funny, Miss Comedian." He shook out his own uniform—one with pants. "You take the lav, but lock both doors, it is shared with the apartment next door."

I frowned at him before entering the bathroom. The room was very tiny and held only a sink and a toilet. Above the sink was a small oval mirror and if the reflection of my head was any indicator, I must look an absolute mess. Vadim didn't look so bad, I thought, but Vadim had a buzz cut. My hair lay in a lanky, tangled bob around my face. I changed into the huge dress, washing myself briefly as I went along. Once I was finished, I went back into Vadim's room. He was already changed and looked very upright and professional in his khaki uniform.

"Can you do something about the size of this thing?" I asked while flapping my arms. The fabric of the sleeves were so loose they billowed like a pirate's puffed up sleeves. "And can I borrow a brush for my hair?"

Vadim came towards me and muttered an incantation for shrinking. Then he touched each section of the dress and under his touch the fabric reduced until it got to a size more appropriate to my proportions. The dress still fit horribly, but at least it didn't billow around me like a swimsuit cover dress.

Vadim cleared off his dresser until he found a brush.

"You never answered my question." I stated as I yanked the brush through my tangles.

"Which question?"

"The one about the girlfriend or cross-dressing."

"Well, if you insist on knowing," Vadim leaned comfortably against the dresser and watched me prepare myself. "Its left over from a covert operation about five years ago. And yes, it was me that wore it. I kept meaning to throw it out, as I do with about half of the stuff in this room, but I never got around to it." He smiled at me, "Good luck for you now."

"I don't know about luck." My hair was too far gone to fix right away, so I just pulled it back into a too-tight bun and stuck a pencil stub through it. "I hope you don't mind that I'm taking what's left of your pencil?"

"By no means, please treat it as if it were your own." I rolled my eyes at him. "I contacted Comrade Ignatievich. They are expecting us. But from the look on his face, I don't think we are going to get much help out of the operatives that are investigating."

He looked at me as if he were waiting for my sarcastic answer. I decided to disappoint him. "Are we ready?"

Vadim took my hand, "Let's go." We had been in the apartment less than twenty minutes.

The next place we arrived was a sealed room. There were two doors, no windows, blinding white walls and fluorescent lighting. I had to blink my eyes a few times to get used to the harsh light. Next to one of the doors was a doorbell button. Vadim pushed it.

"That door," he said pointing to the door opposite them, "leads nowhere. I think there is a masonry wall behind it. This door is the entrance to the Cosmodrome operations center for 'special' visitors. Whoever answers this one thinks we have come through a special underground entrance." He laughed. "They will think we are big shots."

I turned to look at the other door. "By the way," Vadim continued, "Has your Russian improved any in the last decade?"

I eyed him with wrath. It had always been a sore subject with me. While I spoke French, Italian, German and English fluently, I had always struggled with Russian. "A little," was all I answered.

"Well, since we don't have time for a language charm, let me do the talking," he returned smugly.

"As if that will be of any help. You've never been a smooth talker." I replied petulantly. We were acting like 12-year-olds again.

The door with the doorbell opened with a long creak. The attendant on the other side was already saluting. Vadim stepped through and nodded at the underling. "I need to meet with the head of security regarding the earlier breach."

"Yes sir!" Once I was through the door, the underling shut it and bolted it, then led his two 'special' visitors down a maze of undistinguishable hallways. All were painted a graying white and lined with fluorescent light strips. The dinginess of it made me want to gag.

After a short stairway up we arrived at a security door. The guard there was less impressed with the way we had entered the building. He examined us closely and asked lots of questions. When the guard seemed satisfied, he handed us over to yet another guard to lead us to yet another security door. At the fourth such door and after many nondescript hallways and stairs leading both up and down, we arrived at the security detention offices.

The wait at our final destination was even longer than the whole time it took us to go through the three previous security check-points. At last we were shown into a room with a large round desk. Again, the walls were white, but at least these were decorated. The flag of the U.S.S.R and a portrait of Kruschev. We each took a seat when left alone in the room.

"Can't you people use a little color here and there?" I started out sarcastically. Vadim ignored me.

A second later the door opened up again. A large woman in her 60s entered the room. Vadim stood and saluted. I guessed it was a superior officer.

"I am Comrade Gostinkov, special KGBB attache to the office of Baikonur. I am in charge of the captives and their interrogation." The woman sat heavily in a chair and folded her hands on the table. "I understand you are Vadim Nazarova, KGBB Agent-at-large, and this is Esmeralda O'Rourke from our esteemed U.S. counterpart AMIS." I nodded at Gostinkov.

"I understand that you wish to interrogate the two Arcani-mus agents that were apprehended prior to this morning's launch."

"Yes," Vadim and I responded in unison. I added, "I would also appreciate a chance to examine the container they were trying to load into the rocket."

Comrade Gostinkov looked me over as if she were examining a rotten tomato. She took her time in responding. "I shall look into the matter." She looked back to Vadim. "We are in the process of interrogating the prisoners at this time. However, I believe it will be possible for Miss O'Rourke to have a turn with them once we are finished." She rose from the table. "Now if you will follow me, you can wait in the office lobby."

She led us out a different door and into a small room that held a desk, a young woman manning the desk, and six chairs lined up against one wall. On the wall opposite were four doors. Gostinkov indicated that Vadim and I should wait here. "Have a seat for now. We shouldn't be too much longer."

"While we wait we could take a look at the container," I asked hopefully. Gostinkov turned to me with a look of such disdain, I couldn't help but wonder if this woman had been raised as royalty in her early years. Before Gostinkov answered, her eyes flickered for just a second to the door on the far right.

"That matter has not yet been decided on. You will have to wait and be patient." She turned toward the left wall and farthest door. She stopped at the desk and spoke quietly to the young woman. She left the room through the last door.

"Now what?" I asked Vadim taking a seat randomly.

"Now we wait," Vadim answered and sat on a seat one away from mine. The girl at the desk watched us closely, probably the last minute orders from Gostinkov as she left.

From the clock on the wall, I realized that it had been over an hour since we had arrived at the Cosmodrome complex. Time was running out for the Cape Canaveral launch.

Knowing that the woman attendant would likely only speak Russian, I began to talk in Italian. Before Vadim had even had a chance to respond, the attendant demanded that we be quiet, "Niet."

Each of us shut our mouths and sat silently staring at the wall opposite. Now and then Vadim would drum his fingers or I would smooth back my hair. Our attendant sat resolutely at her desk, hands folded in front of her, watching me and Vadim as if we were the prisoners.

I was very bored. For the first forty minutes or so, I let my mind wander down memory lane. A place I didn't usually care to go. I quickly got tired of remembering all the wonderful, fun, exciting, and stupid times that I had shared with Vadim growing up. I wanted to talk to Vadim, since he was sitting right there next to me, but I also didn't want the nosey attendant to know anything—important or not.

I was thinking of different spells I could use to block the sound or make it seem as if we were staring straight ahead unmoving while we moved all we wanted. But the guard, who was obviously a witch of low rank and talent, would be on the lookout for obvious spells. Then I remembered a trick Vadim and I had used when we were very small. It was one of my first magics. Before the War, I often toured with my mother and her opera company. It was the same company where Tola worked as seamstress. During performances, Tola watched the kids backstage where she waited in case of any wardrobe problems. We children were supposed to sleep on the little cots that Tola provided for us, but with a live opera taking place in front of packed houses, not 20 feet away, it was a near impossibility for us to sleep—at least before the second or third act.

We were not allowed to play backstage but instead invented quiet games to play while we laid across our cots. I discovered first how to make light letters and pictures with my magic and soon had taught Vadim as well. We could write and draw across any surface and with a snap or a wave the light would disappear. Later we even learned to write in the air and would leave cheeky messages for Mistress when we were in her care.

I had to think about it for a minute to get it right. It had been many years since I had even thought of it. It wasn't a hard spell, or even a spell, but there was a trick to getting the light to stay in place. When thought I had remembered it correctly, I shifted a little, crossing my right leg over my left, so that I could quarter turn towards Vadim without looking as if it were on purpose. I looked up at the attendant as I moved and was greeted with a stern, unmoving look. I began to write with my left hand, the writing a bit shaky, on the seat between us.

Vadim had been leaning his elbows on his knees, his chin in his hand when he glanced sideways at my moving fingers. "Remember?" I had written. Vadim sat up too quickly and had to assuage the attendants watchfulness by slumping in the other direction and staring at the opposite wall. He put his right hand down on the chair. He swiped at my message and wrote: "Of course, glad you thought of it. Bored to tears." Although he did not spell out tears, he used a teardrop to symbolize it. When the two of us had used this method of communicating as toddlers, neither of us could spell very many words, so we often used pictures in place of letters.

"What now?" I wrote next.

"?" Vadim answered, then quickly erased it. "Stalled, won't get out in time."

"Yes think so too."

"Checkers?"

I had to steel myself to keep from snorting out a laugh. I drew the squares.

It was slow going. While Vadim didn't have to look down to write responses to me, he did have to look down to make sure he knew how the game was being played.

Half way through the game, he paused and then winked at me. Above our makeshift board, he wrote "remember this one?"

He turned to face the woman at the desk and screwed up his face and shut his eyes in an exaggerated way. I could just make it out. It took my a few seconds before I realized the spell–Blinky. When Vadim blinked, so would the attendant, except that her blinks would last five or six seconds. She wouldn't know what she had her eyes closed for so long. I nearly snorted out loud. We had come up with lots of silly spells to pass the time in classes and while biding our time until one of Mistress's lectures. That was one of the silliest.

When the spell had taken hold, Vadim turned back and played his next move, then looked up at the far wall. The attendant opened her eyes. She hadn't noticed anything. The magic we were using added up to nothing more than children's pranks, but it felt good to use magic–however small.

We played our game for a long time, both of us trying very hard not to look at the clock too often. In the middle of our second game, I felt a vibration from the necklace. Mistress was trying to contact me. I glanced around trying to figure out how I could talk to Mistress without the attendant knowing. I felt sure that if I asked for a private place to make a communication, I would be monitored.

I wrote above the checker board, "Sound wall between us" and grabbed my necklace for emphasis.

Vadim blinked and then turned to me and nodded. "After the next blink," he whispered so low, it was nearly silent. From the corner of my eye, I saw Vadim shape the spell in his hand. He blinked again and I saw a opaque swirl extend from his hand and form a clear, concurve barrier around me. I stretched and then recrossed my legs the other way so I had my back to Vadim and the attendant.

"Mistress," I called quietly into the mirror.

"Its about time," Mistress replied, her face sliding across the tiny mirror.

"Keep it down," I demanded.

"I'll speak at whatever volume I choose," replied Mistress, although she did lower her voice. "Where are you? Have you interrogated the prisoners yet?"

"I'm in a waiting room outside where the prisoners are being held. At the rate its going I don't think we will let me in to see them before the Cape Canaveral launch."

"What a petty game these Soviets play. As if stopping Project Iris wasn't important to us all. What about the package?"

"Not a glimpse. Although I have a feeling it's in a nearby room."

"I give you 15 minutes to see what is in that package, then report to me. I need you at the launch ASAP."

I turned to face the opposite wall again. I blinked hard to let Vadim know he could release the barrier. He blinked while letting the spell go. I erased the checkerboard and wrote on the seat. "Need a 3 minute distraction, going invisible."

"?" Vadim wrote back.

" ↑ the package, distract while go → door."

Vadim wrote a check mark to show he understood. I took a deep breath and began concentrating on the invisibility glamour. I cradled it in my right hand so I could throw it over myself at a moments notice. When the spell was complete, I got up and walked to the attendant's desk.

"Where are the restrooms?" I asked in my rusty Russian.

"Out that door, take a left, take a right at the next corridor and it is the last door on the right. You will see the sign." The woman pointed as if that was a clear indicator of where to go.

"Thank you."

I opened the door. Once out in the hallway I checked to see that no one was around, threw the spell over myself and walked back through the open door.

Vadim was already at the attendant's desk, readying himself to flirt with the attendant.

"Thankfully that American is gone for a little while, now us countrymen have a chance to talk."

I wondered if he used a charming spell on himself—the woman looked a little dazzled to be spoken to in such a manner—or if we was really that handsome and charming to every woman. I attempted to not listen to their talk while I walked across the room to the door Comrade Gostinkov had inadvertently looked at while talking about the package. It could very likely be a trap, I told myself, but Gostinkov determinedly did not look clever enough to think of a trap. A bully, yes. A plotter, no.

At the door, I tried the handle. It swerved smoothly, but did not budge. It was magically locked. I looked over at Vadim, who had leaned over the corner of the desk. The attendant could still see the door, but the bulk of her field of vision was taken up with Vadim.

I used the simplest of unlocking spells—I drew an incomplete infinity sign around the handle. When I tried again, the latch gave way. Double checking to make sure the woman was still occupied, I eased open the door, darted through and shut it quietly.

I found myself in a small storage room with a large delivery door at one end. A single row of florescent tubes lit up the place. The walls were lined with rude shelves and old wooden boxes. I didn't have to search far to find what I was looking for. Taking up most of the unoccupied floor space was a large crate—five feet by ten feet. The nails had been removed from the top and the lid laid across it, slightly askew.

I raised up the heavy lid and peered inside. A large cylindrical metal object lay inside. It was only about three feet in diameter and five feet long, but there were a number of protruding stakes and a big oval screen as well. The outside matched up to the diagrams that Dr. Perrin had given to me. Now I had to find out if it was the true satellite with the Oracle stone inside.

The object was far too heavy to lift, so I climbed into the box. The object was definitely had strong spells attached to it. I could feel them emanating from every surface. It took me a few moments to locate a hatch to look inside. The hatch was welded shut. I had to do some fancy coaxing to get the metal to release itself. Finally after a couple of misspells and one correct one, I got it off. The hatch opening ran nearly the whole length of the satellite. I recoiled in horror when I saw all the wires, gizmos, and machinations that filled the interior. At least I knew what I was looking for. If I hadn't, I would have given up instantly.

I needed to find an inner box that would house the stone. I broke off one of the exterior spines of the satellite and began poking at the bottom. I prodded and searched, sometimes having to dig in between gadgets to see what my probe had hit.

Near to the top I found a panel not covered with wires, but latched shut. "Sort of like a battery casing," I thought. Pulling open the latches, I found an empty interior. There were all sorts of wires and junk on the inside that led to the rest of the machinery outside the casing, but there was no Oracle stone.

That was all the proof I needed. I hauled myself out of the box. Straightening out my glamour, I headed for the door. I hoped Vadim still occupied the attendant. I made my exit as quick as I could, but I needn't have feared. Vadim was still leaning over the desk talking to the attendant. It looked as if the poor woman was ready to don a dress of white and stand at the altar with him. This only gave me a small pang of jealousy. I had other business to attend to.

The door to the hallway was still open. I dashed through and removed my glamour. I needed to get out of this place quick, but knew I couldn't jump so near a magic prison. I needed Vadim for this and the attendant was not going to be happy. In more ways than one.

I stormed through the door. Both Vadim and the attendant looked up at me in surprise.

"We need to take a walk right now." I grabbed Vadim and pulled him into the hallway.

"Stop! Stop! You aren't allowed to leave. Stop!" cried the attendant, but it was too late. Vadim and I had taken off down the hall. We could hear an alarm sounding.

"They have alerted the soldiers. We won't be able to get out any of the exits now."

"The satellite was a fake. There was no stone and no magic. I've got to get to the U.S. now."

"Not to worry. By the time we get to the next floor, we'll be far enough away for you to jump. I'll distract them."

I was going to ask how, but I heard the sound of running coming up behind us. Vadim and I increased our speed. We hit a stairwell and began to climb at a run. About halfway, Vadim grabbed my arm to slow me. "At the landing take off."

"What about you?" I asked as I kept going.

"I can take care of this."

Just then I reached the landing. I turned to jump and saw a stunning flash where Vadim should be, but it was too late for me to go back. I was already at headquarters.

"Damn him!" I shouted running down the entry hall. The attendant on duty, a teenager I didn't recognize, attempted to stop me but was too timid to try.

"Tell Mistress I will be in her office in less than a minute."

Chapter 13

Cape Canaveral, Florida

July 2, 1959

Mistress was just coming around the side of her desk when I burst in. Mistress steadied herself on the table and held a small box in her other hand. She took a quick look at me from head to toe.

"This will never do." And she snapped her fingers.

"What?" I began to say when suddenly I was hit by a gust of wind. When I got my breath again I found I was wearing a uniform that resembled those worn by air hostesses. "What is this god awful thing?"

"You can't go into the heart of Cape Canaveral dressed as a Soviet lackey."

"But did you have to do a quick change on me like that?" I frowned. "I can change myself these days."

"We are in a hurry."

"Yes we are," I turned all business. "The satellite brought to the Cosmodrome was definitely a decoy. There was no Oracle stone. Vadim helped me get out of there fast, but he had to stay behind."

"I knew Himiko would play the Soviets against us." Mistress sniffed angrily. "However, I have our best down at the Cape at this moment inspecting the place from bottom to top. The team is being led by Agent Harker." She handed over the box she was carrying. "Everyone has been issued these."

I opened the box and found a pair of black horn-rimmed glasses. "What on earth for? These are hideous."

"Very funny, Miss Fashion Model. Put them on and see for yourself."

I did what I was told, despite the protest that formed on my lips, and looked at Mistress. Mistress now had an aura of white, a white so intense that it obfuscated her whole person. Looking around I saw that many of the objects in the room had taken on a similar glow—the mirror behind the desk, the panel of buttons and levers on the desk itself.

"I get it. They are magic viewers. How fun!"

"Now is not the time for fun. I had Development make up a dozen of these on the fly, so I hope the magic lasts. I am also hoping that Himiko hasn't disguised the box. Even if she did, you should still be able to see the witches who will be handling the satellite. They are almost certainly going to load the thing themselves."

"Got it," I responded as I looked about the room, looking for hazy white objects. The portrait of Mistress that hung behind her desk glowed intensely. For a split second, I wondered why.

Mistress had moved back to the other side of her desk and had sat before the mirror. "Hettie," she called. While she waited for Agent Harker to respond she turned back to me. "You are to go to the loading elevator. I'm afraid Arcanimus will get through all our defenses. You will be their last barrier. I'll send you directly to Agent Harker and she can show you where to go."

Just then Agent Harker appeared in the mirror, she wore a uniform identical to mine.

"I'm sending Agent O'Rourke in now. Standyby." I had come over to stand next to Mistress. This was a safer form of jumping if you didn't know where you were teleporting to, but I hated it. The dizzingly blurry part of the leap was made so much worse when you weren't in control. Mistress took my wrist and put my other hand to the mirror. I was jerked like lightening to Florida landing precariously close to Hettie. So close, in fact, that Hettie had to grip my arms to keep me from toppling.

Hettie was standing at the top of steel staircase outside a large warehouse. If I had toppled, I would have had a long fall.

"Steady there Esme."

"Got it Hettie. Anything yet?"

"The payload was loaded onto the satellite yesterday afternoon. We've been monitoring all the entrances since 8 p.m. last night. Mistress herself put a barrier alert up, in case Arcanimus jumped directly in."

"If Mistress did it, then it should be really secure, but Himiko could probably break it."

"I know. We've got six agents on the ground but haven't seen anything. Not even with our special glasses." Hettie winked and touched the frame of her fake glasses.

"How many agents do we have?"

"Eight, including you. I had two agents at each entrance, but the launch is in less than 70 minutes and all the entrances have been sealed by the army. We're combing the area in groups of two according to this chart Mistress made up."

"She said I was to man the loading elevator?"

"Yes," Hettie turned to face the rocket launch. "The elevator entrance is at the bottom of the red steel structure that supports the rocket." See pointed to the right of where we were standing. "You can just see the tunnel entrance to the elevator right there." She pointed to the base of the structure. The launch pad was about a half mile away from the building we at. The Ground Control buildings were off the left. I thought we must be at one of the assembly warehouses.

"I see it." I looked around to see how to get there. "Do I just take the stairs?"

"Yes, but you'll need a pass," Hettie felt the pockets of her uniform until she found what she wanted. "Here. Its an all access badge." She held out a small laminated square that was stamped with an official looking seal. She clipped it to my collar, to imitate her own look.

I started down the stairs, but turned back for one more question. "How do I reach you if I need anything?"

Hettie put her hand to her lapel and held out a small pin. "I've got my mirror on me."

"Me too," I turned and raced down the stairs.

I reached my post five minutes later. The elevator structure was crawling with technicians. It was just more than an hour until launch time. I looked each technician over with my glasses looking for any sign of magic. There were a number of crates and boxes at the base of the launch that were being slowly removed as the technicians came and went in the small trucks they used to go the long distance between headquarters and the launch pad. I started by looking into them, but was remanded by a surely technician in his fifties.

"Sorry, sir," I apologized. I took up a post next to the entrance and watched. 48 minutes to launch. I had overheard some of the technicians complaining that everything needed to be completed by 30 minutes prior to launch. Hettie checked in with me twice, but there was no sign of any magic.

Thirty-seven minutes to launch. I was growing nervous. I had a very strong feeling that the Arcanimus had already slipped past. At 35 minutes to launch the last mini-truck was being piled with the remaining debris that littered the base of the launch. Another truck pulled up and two technicians unloaded a small box with rope handles. It must have been quite heavy, for it took the both of them to handle it. They went up the elevator. At 33 minutes to launch the debris was removed and the second to last truck left. No sign of magic anywhere.

I looked up to the top of the launch and saw the elevator beginning its descent. In another few minutes the last two technicians departed.

"Now what," I said to myself. I walked away from the base of the launch and examined the structure. Nothing moved, no sign of any person.

I pulled out my mirror necklace, "Hettie, anything?"

A moment later Hettie responded, "Nothing. This is making me very nervous, Esme. Anything we can do now?"

I looked around at the empty area. "I don't know." I saw a security car detach itself from the side of a building a quarter of a mile away. "I'm going to hide here until just before the launch, just to be sure. Security is coming for their last sweep, so I'm signing off now."

I dropped my mirror necklace into my blouse and ran up the first flight of the metal staircase. I laid down on the platform and flattened myself to it. A few minutes later I heard the car drive by slowly before me. I waited a minute longer before standing up. My watch indicated that it was only 12 minutes to launch. As the rocket engines began to warm up, I was ready to give up.

I stood up and adjusted the glasses, taking one more sweep of the area. The hot wind generated by the engines drying out my eyes. Finally, I glanced up the stairwell and saw a quick streak of the tell-tale white light. A witch was on the upper platform.

In a second I had made the leap to the platform directly under the top platform. Listening, I heard movement above me and it sounded as if there were several people. I looked out from the platform I was standing on and saw that the whole of the upper level was surrounded with the magic light. They had spelled the whole thing.

"Damn Himiko," I muttered to myself as I began to inch up the last set of stairs. Closely listening to the footsteps above me, as much as I could over the increasing blast of the engines below.

Near the top, I poked my head over the platform for the briefest of glimpses. I saw nothing but some faint glows that seemed to be floating above the platform. "Damn, damn, damn, invisibility spells." I spoke aloud now, for the sound of the engines was deafening. In my hand I began to form a spell of revealing. A glow of bright orange formed in my palm and then quickly solidified into an opaque color.

I ran up the last few steps and threw my hand out as I spun around. A thick orange liquid-like stuff spilled from my palm and shot out in a large circle around me. When I stopped I found myself being stared at by three orange-splattered figures. I smiled at them. The orange liquid had broken their invisibility and marked them as targets. I was going to get a good fight this time.

Also broken were their glamours. I watched as they turned from lab-coat wearing technicians into three young witches. Himiko was one of them.

My smile turned to consternation when I saw Himiko's form appear. I didn't know if I could win a fight against Himiko, but I was going to give it my best.

In an instant I had surprised Himiko's two assistants with stunning blasts. The first hit its mark true and the witch crumpled to the ground. The second glanced off the other witch, only enough power to disorient her. The engines really began to blast then, the platform shaking as the launch time neared.

Then Himiko was at me. She barely moved a muscle as her hands sent a spell at me. I dodged it and jumped to the space behind Himiko trying desperately to work a binding spell on her in the few seconds I had. It wasn't enough. Himiko twisted around, grabbed my arm and meant to fling me to the ground. I was too quick and spun out of the grip, but now our fight had become hand-to-hand combat—my specialty.

Himiko and I grappled like Olympic wrestlers. Stunning sparks kept flying by me as we moved from one stance to another. The second witch must have recovered and was trying to help Himiko without hurting her.

A huge blast shook the whole structure. All three of us thrown off balance. The launch was just minutes away. I was desperate to finish this. Struggling with Himiko, I saw out of the corner of my eye the second witch drop. Vadim appeared behind her. In the second of seeing him, a small spark of hope lit in me and I put in new effort to overcoming Himiko. Vadim moved in closer looking for an opening when a spark of light hit him.

A fourth witch revealed herself. I had missed one with my revealing spell. Himiko released me and jumped back breath-less and laughing.

The fourth witch dragged the unconscious Vadim to the payload doors of the rocket. She magicked them open and tossed Vadim in.

"Out of here now," screamed Himiko to her assistants. In a flash, she had grabbed the two unconscious witches and jumped. The fourth witch followed closely.

I was paralyzed, my mind frozen. Then almost without knowing what I was doing, I ran for the payload doors. I flung them open. Vadim was just inside the small cramped space, laying at an awkward angle. There wasn't so much a floor as a tangle of steel struts and wiring. As soon as I got to Vadim, I saw that also inside was a satellite, secured to the struts, that exactly matched the fake I had found in Baikonur.

In the next second I was flattened against the make-shift floor and Vadim as the rocket launched. The next ten seconds felt like the longest of my life. As the rocket hurled itself towards space, I didn't have time for leisurely thoughts.

My thoughts were a jumble of despair and resignation–I was glad that if I were to die it would be at Vadim's side. I couldn't let Vadim die. I couldn't let myself die, not without knowing what happened to my mother. I couldn't die like this. It would be mortifying when Mistress found out. I had to do something, but magic doesn't work so well in the air when being shot into the atmosphere at hundreds of miles an hour.

This was my last thought before I remembered that the Oracle stone would be nearby. Gingerly I summoned a spell in my hand and found that it worked perfectly. I could move fairly easily once I had cast a bubble of resistance around me. I was delighted to find that in a g-force event, the bubble gave me a tiny bit of freedom of movement.

I had to get the Oracle stone from the satellite. I found it easier than I supposed. The stone hugely amplified my magic and I barely had to snap my fingers to get the satellite casing open. Inside, instead of finding a massive bunch of wires, I found all the parts orderly and the wiring bundled up into neat ropes. This made much more sense than the jumble of parts I found in the fake satellite.

In nearly the same position as the fake, was the casing box that contained the stone. It was heavy and bulky, much more dense than its appearance would lead one to believe. I took a rope of magic and securely tied it on the stone and then hauled it out. I reached out to Vadim grabbed his hand and made to jump back to headquarters. The rocket engine gave a large burst and a shock wave hit me and I was tossed just as I made the leap.

Then I was falling towards the earth. My breath was sucked from my lungs. I lost my grip on both Vadim and the Oracle stone. All three of us free falling. I had no magic without the stone this far from the earth, the thin air whipping past me. I fought hard to keep the fear from taking hold of me and to just try and breathe.

Once collecting myself, I spread my arms and legs and faced downward, slowing perceptibly. Vadim was much lower than myself and I tried to dive towards him. I didn't go any faster and was sure that I would lose him until I happened to tuck my arms in. I flew like a missile and caught up toVadim in seconds. He was still unconscious. I got a firm grip on his arm and turned him face downward and then spread myself as wide as possible. We slowed.

I looked around for the stone. I could make out a falling dot several hundred yards away. I tried to aim myself towards it, but had slowed down so much that I watched it fall faster and lower. In another few seconds I gave up any hope of catching it. Fortunately we were far over the Atlantic ocean at this point, so the stone wouldn't cause any harm in landing.

I found that I was falling above a lovely view of the earth. One I had never considered before. I was thousands of feet up in the sky and the earth was coming closer alarmingly fast. My only hope was to gain some magic as we neared the water and to slow us down enough that the impact into the ocean would not kill us. I had at least another minute or minute and a half before this was really going to be a problem. I thought I might as well enjoy the trip. I only wished that Vadim could be conscious for it as well.

I watched as the ocean and shore of Florida became more distinct. I could make out the islands in the Florida Keys. The light blue water around each island was beautiful.

Suddenly, there was a tug in my belly button. The tug pulled harder and then yanked me through space and time and I was in Mistress's office. Then I was hitting the floor of the office with a painful thud. Between the thud that I made and the sound that Vadim made next to me, it came out more like a canon's boom.

I groaned.

"You idiot child. What did you think you were doing launching yourself in a rocket?" came Mistress's usual chiding. "I knew that retrieving spell I put on you when you were nine-years-old would be very useful in future years."

I was suffering from a mixture of shock and pain. I lay silently, unable to move or speak.

"I suppose you lost the Oracle stone? Really," Mistress said in a huff as she rang a small bell, "At least that unfortunate satellite will be unable to function." A door opened somewhere and something on wheels was pushed in.

"I imagine we will be discussing this later. Apparently you are the worse for wear." Mistress's voice had a ring of pride.

I felt hands on me and saw someone leaning over Vadim. His eyes opened and we took each other in. I still gripped his arm and it took two people to release my hand. We stared at each other the whole time it took, then both of us were whisked away to the healers.

Chapter 14

New York City

July 6, 1959

The heat of full summer lay heavily on the streets of the East Village. Even though it was early evening and the shadows were thrown long, the heat was still miserable. I walked along the nearly empty streets to the small grocery two blocks away. I had been home so little in the last month there was nothing to eat.

It was four days since the failed launch of Project Iris. I had been busy with debriefings and UN Security council meetings. That day I had attended Dr. Perrin's memorial in Paris. The Legation arranged for her to be buried with full state honors.

It had been a beautiful ceremony held in Notre-Dame Cathedral. Madame Picard gave a lovely speech about Dr. Perrin's works of genius and her enduring loyalty to France. She spoke at length about what a lovely person Dr. Perrin had been and how caring and compassionate. I smiled the whole length of the service. Dr. Perrin would have hated every minute of it. I was certain that if Dr. Perrin had had a choice in the matter, she would have chosen no service at all.

It was announced at the end of the ceremony that Dr. Perrin had stipulated that a research foundation be structured in her name using her fortune. It would be housed in her home on Lake Geneva. I thought that was the most important thing of all. Her research would continue.

Before returning home, I had jumped over to Prague to visit Peter's grave. It took me hours to find it as it was at the far end of an old cemetery outside the city. I would have like to have gone to his funeral. It had been held while I was on my way to Damascus. I left flowers, slightly glowing and guaranteed to last much longer than usual flowers, on his grave marker.

Back in New York, I took my time walking to the store, despite the heat. I felt relaxed and was having trouble remembering the last time I had felt so. Mistress had given me a few weeks off, pending any magic-induced disasters.

Mistress and I had gone to Paris together. When I arrived at her office we had one last meeting about the culmination of the operation. Mistress had been unusually supportive and complimentary over the past few days.

"My dear, you did a lovely job presenting at the UN Security meeting yesterday." Mistress was adjusting her coiffure, using her speaking mirror as a real mirror. I had hoped that someone would call Mistress right then.

"The India delegation didn't seem so pleased with me."

Mistress snorted, "Only because you lost their precious Oracle. Yet if their security had not been so lax, it never could have been stolen." She turned to look at me. "I daresay it will be dredged up. A magic that strong shouldn't be too hard to locate, even in the middle of the Atlantic."

I hadn't thought about trying to find it. "I guess that is true."

"I would not mind if the thing were not found. A magic that strong requires a lot of supervision."

I didn't have an opinion on the subject. It wasn't my concern until the next time it was stolen. I changed to subject. "Have you heard anything from Vadim or about him from KGBB?"

Mistress turned back to me and gave me a withering stare. "That shouldn't be any concern to you. Afterall, he is an enemy of the state for which we serve."

"Yes, I know," I said with exasperation, "But I just hope he didn't get into trouble for helping me."

Mistress watched me with those uncanny, unblinking eyes of hers. "It is my understanding that young Vadim will be disciplined for directly going in opposition of orders. However, he did aide in the thwarting of Project Iris which reflects positively on the KGBB and gives them a chance to grab at kudos where it is most certainly not due. So, he will be punished for his insubordination, but not severely."

I smiled with relief. When Vadim and I had been healed, he had told me that after I had left him in the stairwell, he had feigned a wound and had been taken to an infirmary. He had escaped as soon as he could and gone straight to Florida.

"I'm glad to hear it. He saved me up there on that platform."

"Yes, true," Mistress responded severely, "Yet I think you saved him more." She paused to survey me once more. "Come now, let's be off. I hate having to say goodbye to old friends, yet it is an honor that she is owed."

I waited for Mistress to stand, but she remained in her chair, not a little misty-eyed. "As old as I am, one would think I would be used to losing old friends." She sniffed and pulled herself up using the corner of her desk. Using her cane she hobbled next to me to the entry hall to make our jump to Paris.

I did my shopping quickly, not feeling up to being in the middle of so many people. I didn't buy very much for I thought I might continue my truncated trip to Jamaica. But I hadn't decided yet. For once in my life I felt like being still. I had had my apartment in the East Village for ten years and had used it as little more than a hotel room.

Maybe this time I would use my time off to just be at home.

A breeze had picked up since I had left and the streets were mostly shaded by the time I turned onto my block. As I neared my building, I saw that someone was sitting on the stoop. In the shadowed light, I could make out a sailors uniform. Mrs. Peterson, the woman who lived in the first floor apartment had her curtains pulled apart and was staring at the stranger.

"Nosy old bat," I whispered aloud.

The sailor must have heard my footsteps for he looked over his shoulder at me. His eyes grew big and he jumped up to face me.

It was Vadim waiting for me. Just 30 feet away.

In my haste to get to him, I nearly dropped my grocery bags, one can falling out completely. I didn't bother to stop for it. I stopped just a foot away from him and smiled up. He wrapped his arms around me and pulled me to his chest, groceries and all.

By this time Mrs. Peterson's eyes must have been popping out of her head, I thought. I pulled away from him and said, "Come on in."

As I went up the stairs I winked at Mrs. Peterson who still held the curtains open, watching us.

Once we were safely inside my third floor apartment, I started with, "I'm so glad you didn't get into trouble."

Vadim reached out and ruffled my hair. "I am in trouble, this is my punishment." I grinned. "I got put on disciplinary leave, so I came here." A brief look of worry crossed his face, "It is okay isn't it?"

I threw my arms around him in answer. Then I realized an important bit of information. "How did you know where I live?"

"Mistress told me. She also sent me this uniform so no one would be suspicious."

I scowled briefly. Mistress must have already spoken to him before she had met with me that morning. Mistress must have already known about his forced leave of absence and given me a corresponding one. That woman was so mischievous. She could have just told me, I thought. But by that point it didn't really matter because Vadim was there with me.

I showed him my little apartment and he helped to put my groceries away. I cleared out a drawer for him and helped him unpack his duffel.

"Do you mind if I take a shower?" Vadim asked shyly. "Then we'll go to dinner. I know this great Russian place?"

"How about we walk to the diner down the street?"

"Even better."

When I was certain Vadim was ensconced in the shower I went to the kitchen—the room farthest from the bathroom—and pulled out my mirror charm necklace from under my shirt.

"Mistress!" I hissed.

A few seconds later, Mistress replied, "What now?"

"Vadim is here." I spoke quietly.

I thought I saw a flicker of a smile on Mistress's tiny reflected face. "Is that so?"

"Mistress, you would tell me, wouldn't you, if there were any way to break his oath of loyalty?"

"I most certainly would."

"Is there?"

"I'm giving it all my effort, my dear. As much as I can spare."

"Thank you," I was choking up, my whisper became even lower.

"Enjoy your time off. I'll be in touch."

I removed the necklace and put it in the nearest drawer. I changed into a nice dress and put up my hair. I took out the emerald earrings that my mother gave me and even went so far as to put on mascara and lipstick.

When Vadim emerged from the bathroom, all pink and clean, wearing a casual suit, he looked wonderful. My heart leapt in my chest. I was so glad to see him that it seemed almost made up for all the years that I didn't. A nagging thought almost came to my mind–what about when he leaves?–but I quickly pushed it aside before it could take root and worry me.

"You look beautiful," he told me. "Are you ready?"

"I'm ready," I replied. I put my arm through his and we went to dinner.